Dystopian Galaxies
Visions of the Future

Anne Elizabeth Winchell

ISBN: 1-9449-6905-9
ISBN-13: 978-1-9449-6905-9

DEDICATION

To my wonderful mom and dad.

CONTENTS

Vega: Weather Malfunction   1

Denner VI: Love Beyond Translation   2

Aranea: Mother Plague   18

Sarat Station: Avalanche   19

Meena: Dreams of Earth   30

Rondo: The Wife and the Ylsin Raid   32

Psychon IX: Colonist Hymn   37

Callista: The Spectral Fields   38

Destiny: DNA Message   45

Earth: The Human Weight of Gold   46

Acron: Apocalypse   62

Topsidae II: Roadside Ethics   63

About the Author   67

VEGA: WEATHER MALFUNCTION

Thunder strokes the atmosphere
Reverberates in sidewalk stalls
Wires pull protectively
Retreat against the sleeting rain
Inward draws the storefront signs
Until the streets are bare

Safe behind the acid shield
Under stalls now turned to guard
Rows of eyes both flesh and mech
Await each crash with tangent fear
Sidewalks sizzle asphalt mulch
The city waits protected

Lightning flash 'gainst tower ridge
An epic siege of human lives
Petrified by rain that burns
'Til city power be restored
Weather bent to human pride
And clouds dispersed once more

DENNER VI: LOVE BEYOND TRANSLATION

Larée claimed the training exercise would help integrate me with my new coworkers, but I suspect she just wanted to give the others a chance to hunt me like the alien sympathizer they thought I was. Larée made it clear that as long as I wore the hat and beard associated with Zellians, I would be considered an enemy. Harmless paint pellets stocked the guns and the team leaders preached cooperation rather than annihilation, but the universal hostility was unmistakable. This was no teambuilding exercise.

The Terran Intelligence Agency considered me one of its most valuable assets, but Dahl, my placement officer, had assigned me to this backward planet under the command of a woman whose parents had been killed by Zellians. Larée had the leadership abilities to control her division but she did it by sowing constant discord to ensure cutthroat competition, and she openly despised Zellians and Zellian sympathizers. In private, Dahl explained that she would treat me like shit, but she was the least likely commander to recognize me as an actual Zellian. Still, a sense of foreboding followed me everywhere, especially in the woods with two teams of armed coworkers.

Once my team settled on a plan, we slipped into the woods. The goal was to shoot everyone on the enemy team without getting shot ourselves. Whoever had the most players at the end of one hour would win. We moved into position and I noticed the other team waiting in ambush. I spoke into my headset quietly but there was no response. I pressed the speak button harder and tried again. Nothing. I couldn't hear anything, either. Leaning against a tree, I removed the headset and checked the batteries. My heart sank. Instead of batteries, there was a heavy magnet with a note reading "sympathizer."

A steady thwack-thwack-thwack came from the brush ahead as my team walked into the ambush. I could have warned them. Was it someone on my team or the other team who sabotaged my radio? Larée had handed them out, but everyone on my team had access during the meeting.

I moved behind the ambush and took aim at the other team. They were focused on their victory and hardly noticed as paint splattered across their jerseys. Even after they realized they were hit, they stared at each other in shock as if unable to believe that they had been outmaneuvered. Six down.

I wondered how many on my team were left. There was no way of telling without the radio. At least five very unhappy teammates had been caught in the ambush, but the other twelve were nowhere to be seen. Caught in a different trap, perhaps, or still out there.

Creeping along the ground, I raised myself just high enough to see two enemies taking aim at a teammate. I fired and hit one but the other dropped and rolled. She was fast; into the undergrowth before I could get another shot. My teammate stared in my direction, confused, then noticed the enemy covered in paint and seemed to realize that he had been saved. His hand went to his radio. That meant at least one other person in the game, hopefully more.

I lowered my breathing to listen for the woman who had rolled away. I could sense her heartbeat a dozen feet away and slid behind a tree just as a paintball landed where I had been. Good aim. With my breathing almost stopped and my hearing heightened, I listened to her rapid heartbeat as she moved closer. I stayed ahead of her. I heard other heartbeats in the forest. An enemy stood on the opposite side of a small clearing. Shooting him would give the woman a brief opening, but the enemy didn't suspect me at all. Worth it, I thought. I lifted the gun and took out another enemy.

She emerged from the trees and pointed her gun at my chest. The actual blast didn't hurt as much as getting outsmarted by a human. I hadn't met her before and she gave me a hand up, as I had seen other humans doing with their victims after shooting them.

"Hi, I'm Anari," she said. "You've got moves. Are you a vet?"

"I've been in war," I said cautiously. "Have you?"

"Yeah, five years on Haroli, Unghar Province."

I felt better. She wasn't like the other children pretending to fight; she was a veteran and knew the consequences of war. Losing to her was acceptable.

"And you speak Zellian," she continued. "You must be the only other person here who does. If you are a person."

My heart clenched and my vision blurred at the edges. I wasn't speaking Terran. She was using simple Zellian, the kind they taught in the military, but her accent was so convincing I had answered automatically, not even thinking about language. Careless. Humans rarely spoke more than one language fluently and everyone knew I was fluent in Terran.

"You know," she said, "in the war we learned that the best way to avoid getting tracked by a Zellian was to stay around other people. That way they have multiple heartbeats to listen to and they have to decide which is more of a threat. Sometimes they choose wrong."

My ears twinged and burned. She had pushed me in the direction of the other human to trick me into firing? She was devious, and extremely intelligent.

"I've met plenty of Zellians in my time. I can see why a Zellian wouldn't want to be identified as such, especially here. I hope we can meet again."

She waved and took off through the forest, gun ready for action, leaving me stunned and winded.

◊　◊　◊

Working in the translation division posed unique problems. On the one hand, everyone hated me and I would have preferred to avoid them as well. On the other hand, I was one of two fluent Terran-speakers on the planet and generous with my knowledge, so my coworkers constantly sought my company. I did my best to put up with their presence because I knew I would never survive on a human planet alone. Even though Terran was the official language of the division, it was a second or third language for everyone else and they did not speak it well. They translated mundane communications that required no real grasp of the language, and never sought to improve their skills. They only wanted easy answers, and I had plenty. It was bribery, but it was protection. I couldn't let myself be isolated. These people had to view me as a valuable asset or they would turn against me.

Still, being part of the group was unpleasant in the extreme. Having people think I was a sympathizer was almost worse than the outright hate I would have faced as a Zellian, or so I felt sometimes. They often felt obliged to congratulate me, but the ways they did so revealed an atrocious lack of knowledge and respect for life.

"I think what you do is necessary," one of the women said to me as we ate. "We should not wipe out alien right away. We need record the civilization and take good part for our culture. They have good ideas. It not all crazy kill-human stuff. But the alien, they need to be killed. I mean, they not human. It is pretty black-and-white issue."

The others at the table nodded and I kept my eyes focused on the bread and meat in front of me. I was surprised when I heard Anari argue the point. She had been sitting at my table regularly since we met in the forest. The first time she joined I was tense and alert, watching my language and hers carefully, determined not to make another mistake. But she seemed genuinely interested in getting to know me, and not just to improve her Terran. I had come to expect and even enjoy her presence the past few weeks.

"If culture have good values and morals," Anari said, "does not that prove people have good values and morals?"

"They not *people*, though, that is problem. Look at recent plague on Terra. Virus cooperates with host body while infects others, then kills. The *cooperation* good, but no one say *plague* is good. We need to wipe it out, and we need to wipe out alien."

"So alien are plague that happen to use good tactic?"

"Exactly," another worker said in a voice that indicated the end of discussion. "We take tactics for our purpose and get rid of plague. Problem solved."

Anari started eating again, unperturbed. I was impressed. Not by her Terran, which wasn't any better than anyone else's, but by her courage. After we finished she approached me and asked if her Terran had been correct. I said no and waited for the usual outrage. The workers hated to hear that their language skills were subpar. She looked surprised, and asked if I could teach her how to improve.

"Well," I said, thinking back to her sentences. "I guess you could start with basic conjugation. That seems to mess a lot of people up. And use articles. They're important."

"Will you teach?"

Zellians were natural teachers, but we rarely encountered humans who shared this trait. She was the only person on the planet who seemed to possess any curiosity or intelligence, the only one who had asked for help understanding rather than sidestepping a problem. Her chocolate eyes sparkled and I found myself smiling.

"I guess I could give you private lessons after work."

"Good. We meet my place," she said. "Twice a week?"

"So often?"

She gestured as though slicing her hand through an invisible obstacle. "I desire Terran. There is position off planet for strong speaker in Terran."

"What makes you think I won't take that job?" I asked.

My voice was light. I was teasing her, I realized. Not too long ago she had stood over me victorious in battle, and now I was signaling interest. I wondered if humans interpreted teasing the same way Zellians did. They must, because she grinned and half-lowered her eyelashes in what could only be flirtation.

"If *you* want off this place, you go anytime. My place, seventeen hundred hour? I prepare dinner as exchange."

◊   ◊   ◊

The so-called Zellian War progressed as wars do. The extremist Zellian group we were all united against launched a successful attack on Terra's moon and introduced a deadly disease. The moon was quarantined, but anti-Zellian sentiment reached an all-time high and I had to check in with my placement officer three times a day. I spent the rest of the time translating as many messages as I could without breaking my cover. I was one of three Zellian-Terran translators specializing in both my species' healing arts and the humans' biochemistry, making me an invaluable asset in the desperate attempt to find a cure.

I had less patience than usual for the humans even as Dahl reminded me that this was the time to show more, and if it hadn't been for Anari I wouldn't have managed. Somehow during our long meetings we had moved beyond formality and entered a friendship I had never expected to find with a human. I listened to her heartbeat carefully, always trying to hear the jumps and starts that might indicate secret plans of deception, but she was straightforward in everything she did. And she stayed near me at work, interrupting conversations when they became too heated, or, if she saw someone headed in my direction with blood in his or her eyes, preventing the confrontation with an overly loud complaint about the damn network timing out again. Very few people in the office could resist joining that discussion.

I sent off another string of calculations and rested my head in my hands for a few minutes. A strange heaviness had been clinging to me lately. Unless the other translators had more information, we weren't even close to finding a cure. I wished the humans and Zellians could work together instead of having to transmit everything back and forth like this.

"Been sending a lot of stuff," Larée said.

I flinched. She was at my shoulder, working her jaw as if chewing something. Her arms were folded, her eyes fixed on my screen. I glanced at my screen, too. Luckily, it was a vague message in Terran that didn't reveal anything. I needed to be more careful.

"Been watching," she continued. "Since our moon got isolated, you have been busy. No one else have been that busy."

"I just translate the messages I'm given, same as everyone else," I said. "You can check the tracking data of every message I've sent. They all go straight to the government."

She scowled. "You have got special clearance to be here, but I'm putting in a complaint. We don't like sympathizer scum here."

She left and I noted with vague pleasure her improving use of the Terran word 'have.' I also keyed an emergency message to my placement officer on my wristband. I waited impatiently until I heard the faint clink of Dahl's reply.

Wait. It may be a bluff. Translate less, in the meantime. Depending on her complaint, you may be transferred in a few weeks.

I relaxed and returned to work, trying to slow down and waste more time. Although I wouldn't realize it until months later, my lack of response to this message set off a wave of questions among intelligence officers who had assumed I would insist on leaving immediately. As I continued my translations at a slower pace, unaware of the interest I was generating, Dahl was instructed to keep a close watch on me and report anything out of the ordinary.

◊ ◊ ◊

"I want to make love with you."

Anari said the words shyly, in Terran, face turned away as if fearing I would reject her. She was beautiful, in ways I never knew a human could be. Humans, I had learned, were covered with a soft coating of fur on their entire bodies just like Zellians, only it was fluffy and nearly invisible on most. On Anari it was black and thick and coarse along her arms, legs, and under her belly button, and I loved how familiar she felt at times. She weighed almost the same as my people, and had a similar build, attracting me even more. And most importantly, she was smart. She loved languages and now spoke Terran better than anyone save me, and had the essential curiosity lacking in most humans.

"We can't reproduce."

"I know," she said with a laugh. "You say that like it's a bad thing. I love you."

"Love is reproduction," I said.

I was still unclear on the difference in meaning between the two words, since in Zellian they were the same. In our society, the ultimate form of love was a child. I had never considered that I might love a human because there was no physical way to create a child with one.

"No. Love is love. If it leads to reproduction, so be it. But love is the celebration of a relationship between two people; it doesn't require a baby. Do you love me?"

"I never thought about it."

She made a strange noise in her throat and rolled her eyes. I raised my hand.

"Let me think about it."

Love was between two people. It was the feeling and action, perhaps? And reproduction was the result? A third person shouldn't be involved in the initial love, even though babies were the eventual result. Could two people love each other and not have a child? A bizarre concept. But the feelings I had for Anari *were* those of love. I wanted to give her a child, or carry her child, even though I couldn't. I wanted to be her mate, her lover, and take care of her and be taken care of. I wanted the world to know that we belonged to each other. We didn't need a child to prove that relationship; the feeling of love was enough.

Anari removed her eggplant uniform to reveal her honeydew skin as she lay on the bed. I had seen parts of her before out of curiosity, but now I sensed that we would touch and share our entire bodies and I realized I longed to caress her and become one with her. I leaned over her, putting one hand behind her head and one at the small of her back.

She stroked my beard and pulled off my uniform to reveal the dense fur on my chest and back. Hair removal on Zellians was temporary at best and my torso and chin grew back faster than razors shaved. I was able to pass as a human because human males had similar hair patterns, and she didn't seem to mind as she ran her fingers through my fur. I kissed her the way I had seen human lovers kiss.

"I do love you, Anari."

"You are the most amazing man I've ever known."

"I'm not a man."

"Well, you are male, aren't you?"

"Yes, I am male," I said with a smile. "But I am also female."

She went still in my arms, body cooling as she pushed me back.

"I think you said that wrong. You're not female."

"I am. We all are."

"Oh, like, spiritually we're all brothers and sisters?"

Now it was my turn to be confused. I had thought that humans were distinctly male or female, but she seemed to be implying that they were not. I studied her body. She had the enlarged mammary glands I knew to be breasts. They were present on males, but never as magnificently developed as hers. The patch of thick black hair between her legs didn't have the fleshy protuberance that males had. She was unmistakably female, and irresistible. I couldn't find anything in her body that resembled a male.

I took off my hat and let my ears fall naturally. They were not ears by human definitions, but appeared in the same place so humans had always called them ears. In truth we heard sounds through what they called the nose, and the organs on our heads were our genitals. Mine were already tender with anticipation. Anari didn't appear surprised to see them, or frightened, and I silently thanked her for accepting me. I gestured at my right ear.

"Here, I am male."

I pointed to my left ear. "And here, I am female. I don't understand what you said."

She stared at my ears, then took my right ear in her soft warm hand. I moaned and sank into her, surprised by her forwardness. Her lips widened in a grin as if she had just discovered something delicious and her hands moved to my other ear as I whimpered in pleasure. Normally we touched ear-to-ear or ear-to-mouth only, but her hands were gentle and exquisite against my exposed and swelling flesh and I rubbed against her ears in vain, not knowing how to reciprocate. She took my hands and lowered one to her breast and one against her groin until I found a sensitive spot that made her sigh and squeal and a hole my fingers fit inside perfectly as she pushed against me and used her tongue to tease my ears into ecstasy.

I awoke much later and found her curled around me, sound asleep. Her heart beat steadily against my chest and the sensation soothed me. My belly tightened and I placed a hand on it. I hadn't expected to become pregnant so quickly but where love is reproduction, the act of kissing releases the egg. It was unlikely I would carry to term, since the egg was unfertilized, but I would fight to carry as long as I could. Children with single parents were born successfully more and more, I knew, as science learned how to compensate for the genetic deficiencies. And the close contact with Anari's genetic material might influence the fetus, though Anari was incapable of fertilizing the egg.

I stroked Anari's midnight hair and thought of a child born from our love, one of my people but raised with a human mother. We would be outcast from human society, but my people would be curious. They would tolerate it. The tightening in my belly ceased and Anari stirred in my arms. I kissed her forehead. The chances of carrying the egg to term in a stressful environment were too low to worry her with. I would wait until the pregnancy was certain.

◊　　◊　　◊

"Why you all wear hats?"

The man chuckled when I stiffened automatically.

"I be on your side, man. I like sympathizers. We need to learn about the aliens so we can kill them. But I never understand the hats."

"Zellians wear hats," I said. "Why do you wear pants? Or a shirt or socks?"

"They be clothing, man. Hats be optional. Accessories."

He sounded the last word out carefully. In his native language he was probably a good speaker. He was also friendly, always sharing office gossip and exchanging greetings when we passed in the hall. He seemed, like so many humans, to be a good person raised under bad influences.

"Hats are considered clothing for Zellians. They're just as important as shirts and pants."

The man looked around conspiratorially. "I hear they have ears like penis, that be why they need the hat."

He nodded, chin sinking into the barest fold of fat. My eartips tingled. Zellians had been so careful to keep our ears hidden from humans. Humans were obsessed with sex and regularly used sexual torture to extract information from each other. We were so much more vulnerable than they. When I was placed on this planet, I had even been given human male body parts with partial function so I could pass the casual daily exam of the men's room.

Anari and I were careful about sex as well, making sure no one could discover what we were doing. We played an audiotape of a Terran lesson so listeners would think I was teaching her the entire duration of our ever-lengthening private sessions. She said I was paranoid but never objected, and even sealed her bedroom window shades in case we knocked them askew. We had been careful; there was no reason anyone should know about Zellian ears being sexual organs.

"We don't know anything for sure about Zellian anatomy."

"Larée sent this video around. You didn't get? An alien be captured in battle. Its hat be removed and it have long ears. When the soldiers squeeze the ears, the beast scream like it be dying. There be no sound, but you can tell. They cut open the ears to see what they be made of but the officer catch the soldier shooting the video and the video end. You be alright?" he added, placing a hand on my shoulder in sincere concern.

"Fine. I gotta go, uh, you know."

I stumbled towards the bathroom and made it into a stall before my stomach hurled its contents into the toilet. My body and mouth were empty vessels, powerless as my stomach completed the action. I couldn't breathe or think as my body violently rejected the image of one of my sisters violated and tortured in ways I had never believed the humans capable of. We would never harm a human like that. Would we?

There was a small group of Zellians attacking human planets with the undisguised goal of killing humans, but the rest of our civilization had united against them and we were working with humans to get rid of them. We recognized that a group devoted to blind hatred of another species couldn't be tolerated. But among humans, it seemed that no one recognized the distinction between the warmongers and the normal Zellians. Why weren't the humans taking steps to fight the humans who attacked Zellians, when we were taking such steps within our own community? My stomach hijacked my body again and I became helpless.

◊   ◊   ◊

I sent Dahl the emergency code and minutes later, an emergency evacuation forced everyone out of the building. The other employees were temporarily dismissed while local TIA agents secured the premises. Dahl found me curled up in the bathroom. My stomach no longer produced any liquids, but my body kept locking in place, forcing out air as my belly and intestines clenched to rid themselves of the fear. Tears ran down my cheek as I felt the small lump in my belly get pummeled; my body was trying to expel my precious fetus in reaction to the fear but I wouldn't let it happen.

"Hey now, easy," Dahl said.

I couldn't control the spasms and barely had time to gasp for air between them.

"What happened? Were you poisoned? Were you attacked? You have to talk. You didn't say anything, just sent the SOS."

"Fine," I managed. He was speaking Terran but I couldn't think clearly enough to answer in anything but Zellian. "Video."

My body clenched again. Dahl cursed and started sorting through a Zellian first aid kit, communicating with someone on his wristband in rapid Terran. Finally he held the wristband out to me so I could hear it.

"Are you poisoned?"

The words were in clear, soothing Zellian. One of my people.

"No."

"Are you injured?"

"Can't stop," I muttered, just before my body tightened into a knot and I was powerless again, focusing all my energy on keeping the small cluster of foreign cells inside me.

Dahl listened to his wristband, taking out a long syringe with faint blue liquid. Still listening, he felt along my ribs – pausing when my body spasmed – until he seemed to find the correct place. He waited until I had just finished quaking, then slipped the needle in. I screamed. It burned but I couldn't move; my whole body was locked again as he poured the fire into my stomach. My fingers twitched as he removed the needle. Inside, the fire lashed through my muscles but they relaxed as it traveled. In minutes, I could sit up and breathe without fear of the terrifying attacks that had crippled me.

"Looks good," Dahl said into his wrist. "All right, now tell me what happened," he said to me.

I shivered. "Someone told me about a video he saw, that Larée passed around. About a Zellian being tortured. Not just tortured, but-"

Sour acid flooded my mouth again and I shut my eyes and fought it. When I opened my eyes I saw pure rage.

"That bitch. That fucking bitch."

"Is it true? Is there a video?"

Now Dahl looked like he wanted to throw up.

"Yeah," he said. "It's true. The army's not perfect; some soldiers had just lost a friend and wanted to make the alien suffer. The video was confiscated, I don't know how that bitch got it, or if she just heard about it and told everyone. You're definitely not safe here. We're getting you out right now."

"No. I won't leave Anari."

"What?"

"Anari," I repeated. "She'll be in danger. She's spent time with me."

"Oh, that friend you've been teaching. I'll put a watch on her, and get

11

her a job transfer later today."

"No, you don't understand. I won't leave without her. I love her."

Dahl stared at me for a very long time while a string of curse words in seven different languages spewed from his mouth. I was impressed by his fluency.

◊ ◊ ◊

Anari's house was empty when we arrived, but the broken door and smashed furniture spoke of a violent emptiness. When I tried to draw a breath, my ribs snapped like an iron cage and forced my lungs to expel what little air I had gathered. I felt the cage crush my heart and the pounding overpowered any other heartbeats I might have heard. I grew dizzy and Dahl shoved me back in the car, where a team waited to take me to the spaceport.

"No," I cried. "I can't leave without her."

"I'll find her. You're in no shape to look. Get to safety and let me do my job."

"No," I repeated. "I won't go anywhere until she is with me."

Again I marveled at his fluency in profanity. Several local TIA agents were scouting the scene but even though I strained to listen, I couldn't hear what they reported. I tried to leave the car but the cage around my lungs and the agents in the car prevented me.

Dahl ran back. "He really wants to come, he stays hidden in the car the whole time. Pleber Square. Doesn't look good. I'm going ahead to try to stop this mess. Protect him."

The humans in the car nodded. One of them grabbed me and tried to force me to the floor but I resisted and fought for the window.

"Let him see, damn it," another said. "It's his girl. No one can see in."

Soon we circled familiar streets and approached Pleber Square. People filled the street and the driver went slowly as I urged him closer. Everyone, it seemed, was heading to the square and I needed to know why. There were several cars ahead of us, and soon cars behind. The agents were talking rapidly in the local language.

"If this turns into a riot there's no way we can get him out."

"Boxed in on the right."

"We can't get much closer. Make sure you keep a good grip on him if this turns ugly."

"I've got an open side street over here."

"How much you wanna bet it's already ugly?"

They must not have known I spoke the language and I was terrified by their assumption that something bad was happening, something involving Anari. *My girl*, the human called her. She was mine, and I was hers. Until she stood my side again, with her curtain of ebony curls and thin, wide smile radiating laughter even as she slept, I would be alone no matter how large the crowd became.

I stared over the heads of the people to the center of the Square. I barely felt the agents' hands on my arms and legs as I squinted. There was a platform. Several hundred people waited now, perhaps even a thousand, and the number grew. I felt something cold on my arms, waist and legs, and tore my eyes away long enough to see the agents shutting a full body cuff on me. They were taking no chances, all right, and no matter what happened now, I would be trapped in the car, completely unable to move or escape. At least my belly would be safe from whatever happened, but I would give up a hundred of my eggs if it meant holding Anari safe in my arms. Even with the cuff, the agents held me, as if fearing the metal wouldn't be enough. I wondered what they expected to happen on the platform. What atrocities was humanity capable of that I had not yet witnessed?

Larée appeared on the platform and began speaking.

"I want to hear," I said. "Open the window, I want to hear."

"You don't," one of the agents said.

"I'll input the sound. We're not opening a window," another voice said.

"Where the hell is Dahl?" a third demanded.

"TIA should reach the platform in five minutes," the second voice responded before the outside noise came crashing in.

"-attack on our government base by an alien. We are searching for him even now. His sympathizer, one Anari Lazurius, has already confessed to aiding in his mission of destruction."

Larée waved her hand and two office employees, people I worked with every day, led Anari forward. I screamed.

Her head had been shaved, and blood flowed openly from the sides of her head where her ears had been removed. My own ears went numb and I convulsed, cracking my head against the car window before the agents could stop me. I was grateful the windows were shut and no one outside had heard or seen my reaction. I studied Anari, my love. She was too far away for me to see her expression, but her stance was one of utter defeat. Her weight balanced on one leg as if the other were injured, and I could see crimson blood in various places along her eggplant uniform.

"Anari has confessed to crimes against the government, aiding and abetting an alien, and she faces the death penalty."

"No," I whispered.

"Yes!" the crowd cheered.

I stared at them, at the mass of humanity around me. They were happy, thrilled, entertained. A few shook their heads and left with disgust on their faces, but most remained. I stared at one man with two children, far too young to have even heard of violence, let alone seen it. Yet the children were chanting, "Kill the alien!" with the rest of the crowd.

I sobbed and my head fell against the window with another crack. This time one of the people outside stared at the car and poked one of her friends, gesturing.

"Shit," one of my agents said, and the engine burst to life and we hustled towards the empty side street.

I heard something whack against our tires and the car sagged, but the driver kept going. People surrounded the slowing vehicle and started shoving the sides. I tumbled back and forth until everything fell sideways. A door to the sky opened and one by one the dazed agents were dragged out. Then I was spotted, lying as motionless as possible. The human's triumphant crow reigned over the hysteria of the crowd as he grabbed my arm and hauled me out.

"Prepackaged," he said, slapping his hand against the body cuff. "Don't have to worry about you running."

For a moment we were on top of the car. I saw Larée on her knees and Anari staring at me blankly with beaten eyes and a blood-soaked, shaved scalp. Dahl and the full force of the TIA massed around the platform and the entire outraged crowd lay between us. Thousands of humans circled me like baby birds demanding to be fed, mouths open, arms outstretched, screeching for a scrap of flesh to call their own. Then the human who had pulled me out of the car threw me to the ground and the birds became wolves.

A man yanked off my hat and I heard derisive laughter as my ears fell out, exposed. I tried to brace myself but nothing could prepare me for the shock of having my most sensitive parts brutally twisted in his calloused fist. There is no description of such pain in any of three-dozen languages I know. Pain like I felt should not exist. They laid me flat on the ground and stamped on my ears until I feared they would explode and the insides spew out like pus from a burgeoning boil. Parts of my body went numb, and then sensation crashed back like a bullet train smashing a newborn asleep on the tracks. My ribs tightened but my screams continued unabated until someone landed on my nose and the world went silent.

A man grabbed one of my ears, a woman the other. They began pulling in opposite directions and a sharp sawing began where my ears met my scalp. I realized they were hacking off my ears and sobbed, but they were tears of relief. I wondered if Anari had felt the same bitter freedom when her ears were removed. The humans severed my ears slowly, and their expressions were of vicious delight. My femininity was removed first and paraded in front of my eyes. Then my masculinity. Humans beat the ears against the ground but I didn't care. They weren't attached; the ears could hurt me no longer.

The hands holding me changed and I was dragged to the edge of the crowd. I vaguely wondered what nightmare these new humans had in mind. I could see the celebration in the Square and occasionally make out the two thin ribbons of flesh flung up above the eager hands. The face of my placement officer appeared before me. I couldn't remember his name. His mouth opened but I heard nothing.

"Anari," I said, or tried to say over the clots of tissue and blood in my throat.

The man seemed to speak and then released the body cuff. I reached for paper and pen. I scrawled her name in careful Terran. He stared at it, then at me as if in shock. He took the pen and wrote a response.

Already at spaceport. Rest.

When I awoke, I could vaguely hear the sounds of the room around me. I was in a bed at a human hospital and Anari was in a bed next to me. She was dead.

I didn't need to hear the lack of a heartbeat to confirm her death. Her skin was waxy and the damage that had seemed terrible from a distance was unveiled in its hideous glory up close. Her ears had not only been removed like mine, deep holes had been gouged into the flesh and her skull was partially visible. I stared at her feet. The left foot was half the size of the right and I remembered how she had stood with her weight unevenly balanced, as if one leg were injured. Or one foot. I was grateful that the rest of her body was covered. I couldn't bear to know what else they had done to my beautiful human love. Only the night before she had been in my arms, helping me practice human kissing as she stroked my ears playfully, and now here she lay, mutilated and silenced forever.

"You're awake," a familiar voice said in Terran. It was my placement officer. Dahl. "I'm sorry to inform you that Anari died before she reached the hospital. We thought you would like to see her before you left, to say goodbye. We're transferring you to a medical ship as soon as it arrives, and you'll be placed on Redon IV until you've fully recovered."

"Redon IV?" My voice was thick and I could barely form the harsh Terran syllables. "That is human planet?"

I sounded like one of the workers I despised but the effort of correct Terran was beyond me.

"Yes, but you'll be completely protected. You're the top priority in the intelligence community. Attacks on our operatives are unacceptable. The other agents you were with are all resting in stable condition," he added.

Somehow I found I didn't care. Even though their lives were as precious as my own, all I felt was an ache in my heart and a tingling in my belly. I stared at Anari. She was gone, but was I—was it possible? The tingling in my belly couldn't lie. The clump of cells had gained its own heartbeat. I would almost certainly carry to term. I stretched my hand toward Anari. Humans claimed to have souls; perhaps her soul had passed from her dying body to give life to our child.

"Need speak to Zellian. Now. In person."

Dahl fumbled his hands together. "Look, I know this could have been handled better. I shouldn't have let you go in the first place. The local agents shouldn't have panicked and drawn attention to you like that. I should have handled that girl without putting you in danger."

"Anari stays with me until I speak to Zellian. She comes on healing ship."

"Anari's dead."

"I know. Contact Zellian. Tell him she stays. Tell him I need Zellian now."

"We can't just contact your people like that," he said, rather nervously. "There are so many rules and regulations. You're under our government's care; you aren't technically a Zellian citizen anymore."

"Now."

I knew that he didn't want to contact my people and have to explain what had happened, but I also knew that I wouldn't survive on a human planet. Dahl had the capacity to contact at least one Zellian; he had proven as much when I was sick. Only a Zellian would know which medicine to prescribe for cascading vomiting and be able to direct a human to the proper injection site. So this officer had at least one Zellian contact at his disposal. It didn't matter to whom I spoke; any of us would recognize my situation. Going to a human planet in my condition was a death sentence.

After several minutes of failed persuasion, Dahl cursed and went to the main screen in the room. The screen faced away from me but the voice I faintly heard was unmistakably Zellian. I couldn't understand the conversation. The officer returned to me as if expecting me to say something. When I didn't, he winced and placed a hand on my shoulder.

"They really did a number on you, didn't they? I keep forgetting you can barely hear. He asked why you want a dead human with you. I said it was because you loved her and he told me he wanted to hear the real reason from you. So why do you want her? You can speak directly to him, in Zellian if you'd prefer."

I answered, and I answered honestly because I knew Dahl didn't speak Zellian. I didn't realize until much later that everything I did and said was being monitored and would be translated within days. Dahl had said I was the top priority but I didn't understand how literal he was being. Unbeknownst to me, the Terran Intelligence Agency, who had been paying close attention to me ever since I had chosen to remain in a dangerous situation, was now focusing all of its resources on solving the mystery of my relationship with Anari.

Previously, humans had assumed Zellians were incapable of forming emotional attachments. Now they were scrambling to determine if I had been corrupted by constant human interaction or if I represented a real dimension of Zellians that they had been unaware of. I was, for all intents and purposes, the *only* priority in the intelligence community. Everything about me was suddenly under scrutiny and if I had known, I never would have spoken so honestly. But lying in the hospital bed desperate to talk to another Zellian, I had no idea that my words would ruin decades of peace with the humans and hasten the declaration of war.

"Sister," I said in Zellian, although in our language the word means brother as well, "the human speaks truth. Anari and I courted and mated, and I wish her at my side so that our union can be formalized before she is laid to rest. And sister, I cannot stay with the humans because our love made me pregnant."

Dahl waited a few moments and I gestured that I was finished, then he returned to the communication. After a few more terse replies that I could almost make out with my blurred hearing, he switched the screen off.

"A Zellian medical ship has been dispatched to transfer you and Anari's body to Redon IV. Due to arrive in twenty-three hours. After that, a representative of your people will remain on Redon IV to assist in your recovery. Do you need anything else?"

I sighed in relief. Once I was on a Zellian ship, they would never release me back into human care, no matter what kind of galactic conflict it caused. No Zellian would ever leave a pregnant Zellian in the hands of humans. Twenty-three hours and I would be safe, or as safe as I would ever be.

"What happen to Larée?" The guttural Terran words ran roughshod over my vocal chords and I longed to speak fluid Zellian again.

"Oh, don't worry," Dahl said with a grim smile. "She was charged, put on trial, and executed."

I gasped. "Killed?"

He nodded with satisfaction. "I told you, attacks on our people are unacceptable. It won't happen again anytime soon."

I watched him leave and wondered how any seemingly good person could rejoice when the death toll for this terrible tragedy had just doubled. Closing my eyes, I prayed for my time among the humans to be over. Anari and our child were my only hope that love could survive in a world dominated by unthinking violence and blind hatred, and though my body was ruined, I would protect that hope with my dying breath.

I wept, in sorrow for the loss of my beloved Anari, in dread of life in a mutilated body, and in joy at the thought of a future with a child born out of Anari's love.

ARANEA: MOTHER PLAGUE

the plague found me
halfway down the corridor
it brushed my hand with a child's shoulder
i shuddered but
it was too late

these innocent carriers
with lucifer smiles
their dna warped to feed on ours
i killed it and
thought of my child

few humans are left
to age and learn love
to fight against the madness of youth
the plague spreads
and we die

i carry it now
my womb spits out poison
children who will never age but hunger
for my flesh
like spiders

SARAT STATION: AVALANCHE

Recorded and narrated by newscaster Lisera Y'Rann. The full video can be accessed in the Galactic Newscast database 32.1.6932 and provides the only record of Sarat Station--Thadre II in the Umon system. Due to the historical significance of this document, additional reading fees have been waived.

The mountains soared in long lines in each direction, circling most of the planet and creating a ravine of dark forest between the two ranges. They were known as the Battle Ranges because they looked like lines of soldiers from ancient wars, facing each other and waiting for the signal to advance. Each mountain in the range was jagged and tall, and looked like a soldier because of the various plateaus sticking out from the slick sides, upside down triangles of earth jutting out like shoulders and weapons on the advancing lines.

I watched the mountains across from me and traced the beginnings of an avalanche as a few rocks began to tumble down the steep cliffs and abrupt plateaus, then larger chunks of earth and dirty snow. The Rebel range was considerably less stable than the one I was on, but an avalanche was still a rare sight. I didn't have enough time to get the camera, so I watched the rockfall with my eyes only. No sound reached me, even though the ranges appeared moments from clashing in battle.

When the rocks ceased, I searched for the camera. My room was an open air plateau connected to the inner station by a single overly large hallway stretching into the rock, and because of the unrivaled views of each of the open air rooms, we had all been given high quality cameras in case something like this happened. We were supposed to keep them out on the sundeck, but I found mine against the mountainside near the plumbing, unlocked and unattached to the weights that the scientists reminded us over and over again were the only things keeping small objects from flying away during the nighttime winds.

The wind felt luxurious in the heavy beds and the sensation of being asleep under the stars with nothing between you and the elements was something I knew I would treasure forever. It was well worth the annoyance of having to lock down everything I owned, and the obligation to record any shifts in the neighboring mountains, and it was already the basis for one of my articles to the *Galactic Newscast*. They wanted articles about the dangers of mining the Battle Ranges, but the editor had grudgingly given me permission to write a softer piece about living on the planet. The planetary tourism board had also expressed an interest, and a financial incentive if my article met their strict requirements. Given the hostility of the scientists toward me and the other visitors, I didn't think my article would have quite enough praise for the board.

The scientists would kill me if they knew I had left their camera unlocked, but luckily I had used it that morning and it had only been at the wind's mercy for a few hours. I returned to the outer edge of my plateau, set and locked the camera, and recorded the mountainside while explaining what I had seen.

As I spoke, another flurry of rocks caught my eye and I twisted the camera on its locked stand to capture a second avalanche. Amazing. I had been on Thadre II only two weeks and already seen what few lifetime residents could lay claim to witnessing. The rocks and snow fell from a nearby cut into the mountain's jagged face, and two plateaus jutted out from the otherwise smooth surface of the near-cliff. Boulders and ice landed on the top plateau and the earth trembled. I was amazed at the strength of the plateaus. It was as though the various peaks of the mountains had opened on a hinge and fallen to the mountainside, only the peaks were still in place and the plateaus were solidly planted.

The rocks seemed to match the strange analogy, too. On the requisite tour, a geologist had pointed out how the newest layers of limestone were lower, not higher, on the plateau, and the lines that told the age of the rocks met perpendicular to the mountain formations. Clearly the plateaus were foreign, yet there they were, and had been for thousands of years: the mystery of the Battle Ranges. The Sarat station was built on a massive plateau with sub plateaus like mine for individual quarters, spread out to provide privacy for visiting guests.

The plateau across from me trembled and the space between the upper and lower plateaus seemed to shrink, almost as if the piling rocks from the avalanche were enough to create a visual illusion. I shook my head and blinked, and stared through the camera before using my own eyes again. They were close, but perhaps I had misjudged the distance initially. The lower plateau was covered in rocks and the avalanche continued around the two plateaus as well, bombarding the mountainside. The upper plateau met the lower plateau and I gasped. There was no mistake now. They were falling, sliding along the mountainside in the groove of the mountain's face, kicking up dirt and shaking even more rocks loose as they sank toward the forest below. I had never heard of a plateau falling.

Low rumbling filled the air, no doubt from the extraordinary devastation across from me. As I waited for the inevitable collision of mountain with earth and the delayed but probably earth shaking crash from the distant event, I saw a third avalanche on the distant slopes, in yet another place. I trained the camera on it, a little reluctant to leave the juggernaut plateaus pulverizing their way to the ground but knowing every earthquake needed to be recorded.

The rumbling grew louder and a rock flew through the air at my left. I turned, instinctively bringing the camera with me. The mountainside at the edges of my plateau slithered. Very small pebbles ran like water through cracks in the larger stone, carrying occasional twigs with them. They piled on top of the larger rocks and the weight eventually knocked one of the rocks loose and sent it plummeting below. I stared at the mountain above my plateau and saw the same. Cracking filled the air and I realized that the rocks above my door, my hallway to the inner station, were crashing to the plateau and would eventually block me from escape. Already, the debris was over a foot high and rocks flew almost constantly. I thought of the plateau across the mountains and how it had fallen and I knew that if I waited, the ground I stood on would break away from the mountain and slide to complete destruction miles below.

I grabbed the camera and ran toward the door. The rumbling was a steady roar now, physical as well as auditory. Rocks fell unevenly and there was no way to predict when one would come. I forced my feet to move and braced myself for the crushing agony as I sprinted into the covered hall. I screamed as something hit my head but luckily my feet didn't stop. When I was protected I put a hand to my hair and saw blood, but it must have been a pebble because I wasn't dead. With the camera still on I recorded the door, now filled to my waist with rocks as they fell harder and faster and the pebbles began pouring in. The hallway around me creaked and the floor shuddered as if desperate to shrug off the new weight. I fled inside.

People massed in the main emergency chamber. Some people pretended they weren't panicking, and shouted reassurances that the station had held for nearly three hundred years and wouldn't collapse today. But they walked back and forth stiffly and jumped at each groan and creak of the rock structure, and their words didn't convince me at all. Most people milled around nervously, comparing stories of the noises they'd heard and their guesses at what was happening. Very few people had been outside and knew for sure that an avalanche was occurring, and no one had proof that plateaus could fall, like I had. The newcomers like me scrambled around the edges, desperate for information, desperate for reassurance that there was a plan, that someone had thought of this, that there was some escape. I wasn't with them, even though I had the same questions. My camera was still recording and I was trying to reach the knot of scientists at the middle to tell them what I'd seen.

I finally approached close enough to hear the end of something before he and the others went silent.

"-might lose the outer ones but keep them calm."

"Can we help you?" a woman said.

"Yes, I was outside filming and the plateaus on the other mountain were in avalanches and were destroyed. We're in danger, too, since we're in a plateau."

The scientists stared at me and I realized I had blood in my hair and was still in the grimy yellow oversuit I'd been wearing all day while researching the mountain mines.

"I'm sorry," I said. "I'm here with the *Galactic Newscast* and I was trained in-"

"Thank you for your concern, citizen, but we have everything under control. While it is true that the other mountain range has been known to react to avalanches drastically," the scientist said in a cold, obviously rehearsed press statement, "We understand our mountain range thoroughly and will evacuate when necessary."

I tried again. "We have to evacuate now! The whole place is going to collapse!"

The woman pasted a smile on her lips. "We were just discussing evacuation. I'll make sure you are in the first batch to leave."

She turned her back and I got the message. At least they knew enough to evacuate. I felt for the transmitter in my pocket and checked the reception. Surprisingly good for being in the middle of a mountain during an avalanche. I edged out of the crowd and dialed my mom, keeping the camera focused on the people in the middle of the room.

My mom's voice was scratchy with distance and I could barely hear it over the roar of the chaos outside and the panic of the people within, but I recognized her instantly and the tightness in my chest loosened slightly.

"Hi Mom. Look, I can't really explain but I love you. I might not make it home this time. I'll keep you on for as long as possible. Is- Is Dad there?"

I heard her say something that sounded like a question and fear and the words I love you.

"Get Dad. I'll try to explain but I want you to know how much I love you, both of you, and how much you mean to me."

My eyes were warm and I knew I was about to cry. I should be learning the details of the evacuation or staying close to the scientists to make sure they remembered that I was supposed to be evacuated first, but none of that seemed to matter. If I died, I died. I just needed to be with my parents first. They were everything to me.

"There's an avalanche and I don't think the station's going to survive. We're supposed to start evacuating but if we don't get out soon it might be too late. You've been the best parents I could ever want. Thank you so much. I love you. Oh, they're about to say something. I'll leave you on, just a minute."

The scientists at the center had to scream to be heard over the double threat of avalanche and mass hysteria but they succeeded. They pointed to tubes along the outside of the chamber that I recognized as the icesurfing tunnels. They said something but I couldn't hear. The crowd began moving and I grabbed the arm of someone who looked like he knew what was happening.

"Groups of twenty on the icediscs," he said. "If it looks dangerous, guides will take us out of the path of the avalanche until everything clears and we can come back."

"But that's not enough, we have to leave now, and what about when the station collapses?"

The man shook his head. "It won't, but why don't you go to tunnel one. They're leaving first and going the farthest. Guests are advised to go there."

I thanked him and plunged into the crowd, who generally let me through without comment when I said, "tunnel one". A few looked at me with sad eyes, as if they thought I was crazy. When I reached the tunnel I saw nineteen people waiting and I nearly collapsed in relief. There was still space.

"This is the one," a voice said. "You're twentieth. You sure took your time getting here, for all your concerns."

It was the scientist, and she didn't look pleased. She shoved me onto the large disc of ice with the other guests, a few of whom I recognized from our flight to the planet. I barely had a chance to strap my feet into the icehooks before the disc began moving. I checked that my camera was still on and I shot a final glimpse of the station as we zoomed into the long tunnel leading to the outside. Then I returned the camera to the pouch on my waist where it would record everything I faced and I scrambled to get out my transmitter. I was on the outside of the ice disc and I knew from my pleasure rides that I would need to pay attention to the orders of the guides to lean and balance my body weight with the others to properly align it and guarantee a smooth slide, but I needed to explain what had happened to my parents. We were still in the protection of rock ceilings. Once we left the tunnel and reached the avalanche I wouldn't have a chance.

"Mom, Dad, I'm evacuating on an icedisc, I'll leave the phone on but I can't talk until we're far enough away. I love you."

I heard my mom over the crash of rocks and the sleet of ice say "I love you," and the warm rumble of my dad repeat the words. I started crying and put the transmitter in my chest pocket.

My tears iced the instant we hit outside air and it was a good thing, because it temporarily blinded me. Based on the screams of the others, I didn't want to know what was happening. Galloping rocks pounded my ears on every side and through the ice I could feel random and rhythmic vibrations intertwining in a deadly ballet. The guides cried out directions for us to lean and I blindly obeyed over the shrieks of air and rock and human terror. As my eyes warmed I saw the rabble of pebbles we rode over and the crashing boulders flinging themselves at random from the sky above and wondered how the guides could remain calm when a single boulder could shatter the icedisc and flatten everyone on it. The other guests and I instinctively crouched as low as we could in the icehooks and I idly realized we had flawless form. I hadn't realized icesurfing required you to be so close to the surface.

It was strange, gliding along the shifting rocks. We could be killed at any moment yet fear was absent from my mind. The ride was pleasure. I braced myself at each rock, of course, and my mind imagined death in excruciating detail, but I felt detached. When the guides called a direction, my body and the body of everyone on the disc changed together, as one, as though we were immune to the fear that I knew was consuming us individually. Our communal strength was great enough to overcome our individual weakness. I was a part of something, for the first time. Because I was on the outside of the disc I couldn't see many of the people but I could feel them and I knew they could feel me. We were together, in a way I never knew strangers could be together.

I heard a scream over the wind and rocks. One of the guides cursed and his voice changed, becoming tighter and higher-pitched. I risked a glance over my shoulder and saw an empty space along the edge of the disc, empty save for a few bloody feet still locked uselessly in the icehooks. My stomach spun and my mouth filled with saliva and acid. But I couldn't vomit; the movement would upset the disc.

The guides called orders faster and we obeyed as the disc spun across the rocks and snow. Large patches of snow were beginning to appear between the sleeting pebbles and hailing rocks and one of the guides said we were almost out. We continued gliding over longer and longer patches of snow until we reached a plateau with no movement at all. I waited for the pebbles to follow us and send this plateau tumbling down, but nothing happened.

"This plateau is on a different mountain than the station," one of the guides said. "It won't be affected by any avalanches on the station's mountain."

"That avalanche was too big," the other guide muttered. "All the others will have to come here too, the closer spots are gone."

At the guide's direction, we unhooked our feet and hobbled off the disc. I went to the edge of the plateau and stared back at Sarat station, lifting the camera. The entire mountainside was in motion and while the station still stood, all of the outer plateaus had fallen. The bottom of the ravine under the station was grey with stone and snow and very few trees emerged amid the wreckage.

The terrible rumbling had quieted as we moved into the snowy area but now we heard a boom, the earth crying in protest. I trained the camera on the station. I thought my hands were shaking at first, but after a few seconds the other viewers gasped and I knew I wasn't mistaken. The station was falling. Sliding. It lowered down the mountainside like a massive nose breaking away from a face flung upside down in agony, leaving the strange flatness of the skull behind, and thunder ripped through the ravine and cracked the sky. Wires and metal were dragged kicking and screaming out of the mountainside as the plateau descended and I wondered if the entire mountain would collapse. The station had built tunnels through the mountain from one end to the other and the structural support for those tunnels was being yanked out like the muscles of the newly opened skull. Would the entire mountaintop then collapse?

"Back to the disc," one of the guides called.

I knew he shared my concern and I was strapping myself in before the others could move. They stared at us, and at the station, now traveling inch by inch downwards toward inexorable destruction.

"Bet if we'd stayed we could have just gone down like an elevator," one person whispered. "No need for all this excitement. Get off at the bottom and be done with it."

The other guide, still not on the disc, nodded in agreement.

"Are you getting on? We have to get out of here now! This mountain isn't safe!"

Again the crowd looked at us blindly, then returned to the station. The guide stared at me, the only other person on the twenty-person disc. There was no way the two of us could escape. My chest tightened and I thought of my parents, and my friends, and my home. Everything gone because these stupid people couldn't see what was happening right in front of them. They were so caught up in the beauty of the destruction, they couldn't see that when the mountaintop fell inward on the soon-to-be-unprotected center, the resulting earthquake would be felt through the entire range.

The guide with me swore and unhooked himself, gesturing me to do the same. He leapt off the disc and started feeling the side of the disc, opening panels that I hadn't realized were there. I had assumed the icedisc was pure ice, but apparently it was more machine than anything else.

"Look, this mountain comes close to another, Trevan Peak, that isn't connected to the Battle Range at all. There's a leap you can make from this mountain. It's dangerous and I've never tried it with anyone else but if we can get to Trevan we'll be a little protected. Better than the ravine floor, at least. Ever ridden one of these before?"

He pulled out a machine vaguely reminiscent of a bicycle, only this one was extremely thick, had an engine, and had ice like the icedisc instead of wheels. I shook my head.

"Same principle as the icedisc except you'll be sitting behind me. When I lean, you lean. Don't let go of me. Now get on."

He sat on the machine and I awkwardly threw my leg over. I adjusted the camera at my waist so that it would film the world instead of him, then grabbed his waist the way he showed me. The other people didn't pay attention to us at all; they were trapped by inevitability.

The buzz of the engine was loud, but not nearly as loud as the avalanche had been and I wondered how long it would be before the quake would start. The station sank slowly, far slower than the other plateaus I had seen, and it would take time for the full weight of the mountain to realize its triumph over humanity's interference. I leaned against the guide and followed his body as closely as I could as we rode across snow through lanes of boulders and trees. I tried to recapture the feeling I had experienced on the icedisc of being part of a greater whole but it was gone. Now I was terrified.

Every time the thought of death crept up, my body tensed and I started trying to guess his movements before he made them, often guessing wrong. He swore at me and told me to relax. I tried, but I kept waiting for more thunder and crashes. It was only a matter of time. I shut my eyes and it helped. I imagined that I was already dead, that he was the only thing in the universe. I tried to imagine we were making love, but that didn't help either. I kept my arms tight around him and moved the way he moved, trying to keep my body relaxed as much as I could, my mind as clear as I could, inwardly flinching at each bump in the path and uneven burr of the engine.

"We're coming to the jump. Keep your eyes closed and hold tight. Grab the icebike with your knees just like you're doing, and don't let go of me. Just do what you're doing."

I had to stop myself from opening my eyes. What was I doing? Clearly I was doing something right, but what? I forced myself to relax. He had told me. I was closing my eyes and holding on with my arms and knees. That was what I was doing right. I didn't need to overanalyze. I felt his body tense under mine and I instinctively followed his lead. The air on my cheek became colder, if that was even possible, and for a moment I opened my eyes.

We were between mountains. I clutched him tighter but didn't flinch. I closed my eyes. There had been nothing underneath us except sky. Below was a forest, not as dark as the ravine, not as deep, but still too far away for comfort. And before us had been a mountain, but not close enough. Certainly not close enough.

My stomach began to lift and my spine tingled and I realized we must be falling. The bike seemed to drift away from me and I tightened my knees convulsively, desperate to keep it. I couldn't be alone in the air. The guide was in my arms, the bike between my legs, and both were hard to hold on to, as if gravity wanted me to let go. I tried to tell myself that gravity didn't care, that freefall applied to all objects equally and couldn't be isolating me and flinging me to a lonely death.

Above the shear of the wind I heard thunder, the feared sound of the earthquake, as it raced from one ear to the other and I imagined the shudders exploding from the station outward to encompass the planet. Could we land if the earth were quaking? Would we land at all? The guide's body was still tense under my hands and he hadn't said a word. The flight had lasted too long, the landing had to be soon. The thunderous roar continued, followed now by a number of crashes. I tried to tell if they were coming from the mountain in front of us but the sound was too great, too hard to locate. It was everywhere.

"Brace yourself," the guide yelled.

I tried to squeeze myself down into the seat and prepare for a hard landing, and I locked my hands around his waist.

The ground beat the bike like a giant swatting a gnat and we ricocheted back into the air before bouncing back again, and again, until the fourth time the guide managed to keep us on the ground. The first landing blasted my pelvis with pain and by the second I couldn't tell if my knees were locked around the bike or not. I held tightly to the guide and after we were on the ground going far too fast, he swore. He grabbed my hands, my arms, yelled at me to let go of the bike, and leapt off the side into the snow. I was dragged along, barely aware of anything beyond the earthquake rumbling all around us and the sudden explosion of light and noise as the bike crashed into a stand of trees. My spine roared with the earthquake and burned with the fire I could see licking the icebike. Dusty smoke filled my nostrils as I tried to sit up and failed. The snow around me was red and I stared at my exposed leg bone in shock.

"Come on, there's a cave nearby, I know where we are," the guide said. "I know first aid. We need some protection from the quake. And the fire."

The heavy smoke was growing thicker and I realized the bike had probably carried several canisters of fuel, now igniting a forest fire. He picked me up and I clung to him helplessly. His guide uniform smelled of sweat and ozone and I wondered how far up we had been when we made the mountain jump. I didn't feel anything as he carried me and soon we were inside a cave and he was straightening my broken, numb leg and doing what he could with the small first aid kit attached to his belt. The belt itself was being used as well, wrapped tightly around my thigh to prevent blood loss.

I could hear the bowels of the mountain aching with the suppressed desire to split open and destroy us, and I wondered if being inside a mountain during an earthquake was the best idea. I glanced out the cave opening and saw pebbles shifting. An avalanche. Another avalanche. Was it safer to be inside or outside? I didn't know. I had always trusted that other people would tell me.

Vaguely I pointed the camera at the opening to record the new avalanche, pleased to note that the device was still functioning. I probably had spectacular footage, if I survived to get it out to anyone. I fumbled at my chest pocket for my transmitter. It was still there but the line was dead. I tried making a call to my parents again but there was no reception. I wondered if they knew I was alive.

The guide finished with me and started making calls into his transmitter. I hoped he was getting better luck. A loud crash startled me from my daze and I stared at the rock in the cave opening. The guide pushed me closer to the back of the cave, as far from the opening as possible, and told me to sleep. I tried calling my parents one more time. No luck. The guide had a grim expression on his face as more rocks began piling up at our cave and I knew he hadn't been able to contact anyone either.

It was possible, I thought, that my parents had overheard the guide mention Trevan Peak; that the transmitter was still functioning then. If they had, they would send help. We would eventually be found. But if the line had died before then, or the sounds of the earthquake made it impossible to hear, then the guide and I would be trapped here until the earthquake was over and possibly even after that, if the rocks blocked our exit. I at least wouldn't be able to leave even if we weren't trapped, since I couldn't walk. I wondered if we could have escaped with all twenty people, or however many were left after the casualties during the journey. Maybe if the scientists had acted sooner. If they hadn't built the station in the first place. If my editors hadn't wanted a story on mining here. If I hadn't leapt at the chance to see the exotic Battle Ranges. So many ifs.

◊   ◊   ◊

The avalanche has finally stopped, and the guide has left to find help. The pain has set in for me, although I feel nothing below the waist. I believe I am paralyzed, and I don't think I will survive long enough for him to return. I don't know why I'm recording the events of the past few days into the camera now, when the camera no doubt shows a far better picture of what happened than I can possibly express, but no camera can capture the human element of a world destroyed. Mother and father, I love you more than you can possibly know. Speaking to you during this tragedy brought me comfort in ways I can't express, and gave me the courage to continue. If I survive, and I still hope to survive, it will be because of you.

I don't know who is at fault for this great failure of humanity, and it doesn't matter. Blame never matters. Everyone is to blame, including myself. All that we can do is make sure this never happens again. The camera is about to die, and I can only hope someone finds it someday. This is Lisera Y'Rann, reporting from Trevan Peak. --

MEENA: DREAMS OF EARTH

Up to twice the speed of light
Galactic warships pierce the night
Defying laws of energy
Like pirates in a midnight sea

Aboard a transport, near the hatch
A slave named Meena strikes a match
Lights a candle from old Earth
Smuggled from their latest berth

Vanilla almond clings to air
Too thick with chlorine, routine care
Her husband makes a feast of food
With soil-grown fruit to fit the mood

An hour of time to share the past
Empires fall, but memories last
When humans lived in unity
And dreamed about their destiny

"To Earth," says Meena in a toast
Missing humankind the most
Scattered now, her people roam
Forbidden from their earthly home

DYSTOPIAN GALAXIES

Generations pass unmet
Culture fades, people forget
The alien becomes the norm
Humanity has lost its form

Her husband cannot understand
His species never lived on land
But he joined in sympathy
He loves her truly, happily

The candle and forbidden fruit
Barely earned with years of loot
Earn a sparkle of respite
A blurry dream of human might

Travelling too fast for light
Humanity's a treasured sight
Elusive slaves on every moon
And here, in Meena's ship cocoon

Then sirens blare and Meena sighs
Inhaling now the smoke of lies
Space was once a challenge braved
Space now held her race enslaved

The Masters who control the stars
And first brought humans beyond Mars
Forbid their memories of life
Spread through time and space in strife

Meena faces punishment
Five times with claws will she be rent
Her husband has a gentler fate
And soon receives a tamer mate

Ten years past light speed flickers by
Before she sees a human eye
She meets his gaze and in her heart
Another dream of Earth will start

RONDO: THE WIFE AND THE YLSIN RAID

Panic. That is an Ylsin raid. Wakened at night by the low bugle you learned about before learning to walk but prayed never to hear. Falling out of your bed, knowing not to light the lantern and bring the aliens straight to the bedrooms. Crawling with the other wives as the keel of the bugle continues unabated. Your nightgown cuts the back of your neck as your knees stumble in the loose fabric but you will not bundle it up to your waist as some of the other wives are doing. They have born children and lost their shame of form, but you are untouched and fear their practiced eyes may find fault with your body, fault that even now might exclude you from the King's suite and send you to an unknown but infinitely worse fate. You stumble with them, bodies touching, a herd of *tandir* fleeing an unknown prey.

On your home planet the stories of Ylsin raids are seared into each child's memory long before the adulthood rite. They are monsters that search the planets for the most intelligent, most beautiful adults. You have heard that they take pleasure in hunting only humanity's finest. You have heard that they wish to eliminate potential human rivals. You have heard that their desire for human flesh is insatiable. When their victims are located, not even the strongest Alliance King can hold back their assault.

The halls echo with the clatter of swords and the hum of strange electronics as you follow the wives silently. Hoarse shouts of enemies seem ready to burst from every shadow but the wives show no fear. Only you are afraid as your hands scramble across harsh granite and your knees swell and jolt with only the thin comfort of linen to protect them from the uneven stones. You want to wail and weep but know it will bring the raiders. You suspect as well that the other wives will silence you long before they arrive, leaving only your body to be found.

In your home before the King's soldiers dragged you from your father's side to join the King's brothel as his youngest wife, your people feared the night of the yearly adulthood rite, praying that none of the new adults were special enough to warrant the Ylsin's attention. The Ylsin never touch children, which you have always found strange, though it won't protect you anymore. You have not undergone the ritual, but being named a wife has made you an adult in the King's eyes. You fear the raiders seek you now. Even if they don't, you stand little chance of survival. In an Ylsin raid, you are killed or made a slave to masters with no understanding of human limitations. It is a longer, more painful death. Many caught in a raid prefer suicide. You don't have that luxury. You and the other wives are property.

The wives slow and come to a halt. You see a dark tunnel at the end of the hallway and recognize the emergency pods. Without a word the senior wives enter the first pod and it silently shoots into the atmosphere, to float harmlessly in orbit until the King calls it home.

The remaining wives look at each other to determine order of importance and you long to jump up and shout, "They're after me, me, let me go on first and they'll leave!" But you remain silent because you are the newest wife, and even though your recent arrival and virginity make you the most likely target of the raid, it also makes you the most dangerous to their own relationships with the King.

Your chest tightens and you can't breathe for a moment, thinking of the wife who had taken your place when your monthly blood had been discovered the first night. The King, furious that his delicate bride would have to wait to be deflowered, had taken another wife instead that night. He had beaten her and penetrated her with enough force to leave her bleeding and battered for hours after she returned. She said nothing to you. None of the wives did. They could not control your period any more than you could, and yet the swollen blood-brown bruise on her cheek is an unspoken lesson to all of you. The King may not control nature, but he controls his wives.

Sounds of fighting draw nearer and the wives enter more pods, casually keeping you out of the early ones. There are so many wives it isn't hard to do and you find yourself at the outer edge of the circle of women, farthest from safety. You want to scream and give voice to the terror in your stomach. You don't. It would bring the enemy.

You weep in silent fear until only five of you remain and they gesture you to join them. You try to move but your legs are locked in a crouch and your arms can no longer drag your aching body across the floor.

"There is another pod," a wife whispers. "When you can move, escape."

The wives leave and as she promised, another pod slips into place. You try to move but are paralyzed. Voices sound nearby and you are surprised how close they are.

"That should be last. Orbit pickup?"

There is a burst of static and a strangely distant voice.

"All escape pods in custody. Still trying to identify target and determine quality."

You taste copper blood on your bitten lip. Which side are they on? Are they making sure the women got to safety, or are they the raiders who had now taken the other wives captive? The King kept his wives isolated and you don't know what his men look or act like, or even what the accent of his people sounds like. You are just a young girl who pleased his eye, taken from a small moon that had only recently acknowledged him King. You know nothing but the ship that brought you, and the wives, and one frightening meeting with the stocky, middle-aged man who had licked his lips when he saw you in the wives' finery, whispering, "Yes, you are a proper bride."

Only your body's blood had stopped him that night, and the four nights since. The other wives wait impatiently for your time to pass, monitoring it closely. Soon, they say, your blood time will match their own. You fear when that happens. You will be a wife then, like them.

"Looks like we lost one," a voice above you says.

A hand touches your shoulder and you jump to your feet. Your body is alive and able to move and you run, run from the hand but men in strange uniforms block the hallway and when you retreat, you find more men, surrounding you. They watch curiously and the man who touched you reaches out to touch you again, again on the shoulder, not roughly but with enough force to keep you from running.

"You're still a child," he says in surprise. "Why didn't you get in the pod?"

Your body is tense and you search for a way to escape. There are five men around you. Their uniforms are crimson and several have blood splattered across the fronts. You don't know if that means they are Ylsinian raiders or the King's guards. Your hands are clammy with sweat and you feel drips forming in the backs of your knees.

"Has the King claimed you? Are you a wife?"

You hesitate. Is he offering a choice?

"What if I'm not?"

He appears amused and stares at your wife nightgown and wife earrings. Your nightgown is torn at the bottom and red from your scraped knees, but you know the King's mark of ownership is obvious.

"We're here to make sure that only the King's property is taken."

"Who are you?"

The man shrugs. "Does it matter? Are you a wife? You can't lie. We can access your records as soon as we return to my ship. Lying will get you nothing but a few hours of freedom, and the consequences will be severe."

"I was to be a wife," you say carefully, wondering if there is a way to avoid slavery if you can just word everything correctly, "But the King has not laid his claim on me yet."

One of the other men steps forward impatiently. "Sir, we know this King wouldn't wait with someone like her-"

"Quiet," the man in charge says. He still holds your shoulder but his hand is gentle now. "If you are here as a bride, why has he waited? My companion is right; your King is not known for his patience. Your age is no reason for him to hold back, even though most would."

You blush and think of the blood between your legs. The flow stopped this morning, although the wives haven't learned of this yet. You were afraid to tell them, afraid that they would send you to the King immediately. You are frightened of him and his throaty laugh and roaming eyes and the way he licked his lips as he examined you.

"It was my monthly time," you say, not knowing if he or any male would understand. They knew so little about women, and desired to know even less. "Please don't send me back to him."

You are surprised that you added the last. You should be more afraid of the Ylsin and the horrors of slavery, not the stocky man who ripped you from your home and destined you to become one of the numb, unthinking wives who serviced him whenever he wished. Tears are in your eyes and you can barely see the man in front of you.

He reaches for a small cylinder in his belt and holds it against your arm. The other man who objected before tries to object again.

"Sir, you can't claim her like this. She's a child, and if she's lying-"

"Are you lying?"

His voice is calm and you look at him for the first time. His eyes are lilac and the pupils are vertical slits, but they appear friendly. His skin is deep bronze, like the others, like your own, but his hair is black like a moonless sky, a color you have never seen in hair before. You wonder if it is natural. His crimson uniform is clean and many gold bars run across the breast, and his stance is confident as he holds the cylinder to your bare arm. He looks enough like you that he might be human, but different enough that he might be Ylsinian. You suspect the latter, but his eyes are so peaceful and kind. It's hard to imagine him feasting on human flesh.

"I'm not lying," you say.

The man presses the cold metal cylinder against your arm. The touch is shocking and you feel a jab deep into your flesh and cry out. He holds your arm steady. His eyes are fixed on the cylinder. You see words flash across the surface in a language you've never seen before and squint to make the strange characters out.

"You are now part of Ylsinia," he says.

Your heart flutters and skips a beat and only his hands on your arms keep you standing as your knees buckle. They will hunt you now, you know.

They will take you to a secret place and hunt you and feed on your fear until they catch you, and then they will feed on your flesh. Is it better than the King and his thick tongue and brutal hands? Is it better than becoming a wife who submits to the King night after night until her mind is blank and her soul is crushed? You shut your eyes and tremble in fear as you realize you would rather be eaten than be one of the King's wives. You will never go back.

"Alright," you whisper.

The man appears pleased and his lips curve into a secret, superior smile. "You may be the first target who has come willingly. It will make things much easier for you. Come with me now, child. The other adults in this place are dead or prisoners. I will explain the truth of the life you are entering."

He wraps his arm around your waist possessively, but with no sexual intention. He is simply staking his claim and giving you support as he leads you and the other men through blood soaked halls, past bodies of men with strange blackened holes smoking through their hearts and heads. You have never heard of a sword that could cause that kind of damage, but you have little experience with weapons or the strange devices of aliens who traveled from beyond Alliance borders.

There is a burst of static and the man presses his free hand against his ear. You can hear words clearly, even though no one is speaking, and you marvel at the technology of the Ylsin.

"Target is still on planet, and viable."

"Already acquired," the man says, seeming to speak to the air. "Target is with me and on her way to the ship as we speak."

He removes his hand from his ear and places it on your hand. His skin is soft and warm and you wonder if all Ylsin are this kind before eating their prey. He is strangely beautiful and you feel safe with him. You will not mind if he is the one to kill you.

"We will wait until you are an adult," he says gently, "before we are married. A radiation disease left the Ylsin sexually incompatible years ago, but our species must be preserved. Only untouched humans are compatible. You will be my wife, my only wife, and our children will be the future."

His smile is confident and you feel a flutter of hope at the thought of surviving and escaping from the King and the corrupt Alliance. You listen to him talk about how you will be educated at the best universities and how his family will adopt you and care for you until the marriage takes place. You might be a prisoner of Ylsinia, but at least they will let you choose your destiny and that is more than you ever dreamed possible. You are still a wife, but for the first time you understand that wife does not mean slave. You smile at your future husband, accepting the challenge of tomorrow.

PSYCHON IX: COLONIST HYMN

Every night, another slow waltz
Lasting nearly to sun's rise
Will tonight the madness take me
Cloak the world in alien guise?

Every night, another victim
Fallen prey to poisoned skies
At first light will I still be here
Safe and sane behind my eyes?

On this night, I beg Your mercy
Forgive us humans for our lies
On all nights I beg Your kindness
I pray our minds are not Your prize

CALLISTA: THE SPECTRAL FIELDS

Her parents died in a shuttle malfunction five years ago and Gina was still recovering from the loss. It wasn't fair; their trip to Callista had been the only space shuttle trip they had taken in their lives yet it was the unlucky one in twenty that malfunctioned upon takeoff and killed everyone inside. Gina, on the other hand, had traveled on shuttles thirty-four times, well, thirty-five if one counted the ride she was currently on. Over half of those times had been in the past five years since her parents died. It wasn't that she was tempting fate or suicidal or anything, but she had thrown herself into her work as a travel writer after their deaths and only by remaining busy could she manage to hold on to the shattered remnants of her life.

She didn't have any friends, at least not true friends. There were some people at the office she was friendly with but she didn't interact with them outside of work. She couldn't have any pets because she was gone so often, even though she knew that pets were often a good way to fill the void in one's life. And romance was out of the question. Her parents' relationship had been so strong all the way to the end, she couldn't imagine finding anyone who would stand by her like that so she didn't even bother looking. No, all she was left with was her job, and she had been planet-hopping for the past five years, boarding each shuttle with a sinking feeling in her gut and waiting for the inevitable explosion that somehow never came. She had beaten the odds so far, but she knew it was only a matter of time.

Gina was especially nervous on this trip. Her editor had finally talked her into going to the most prized destination for travel writers, a planet that attracted droves of tourists yet didn't have a single good article written about it. Her parents had always been obsessed with the planet and its famed Spectral Fields and they had saved up their money for years to be able to afford a trip here. At least they had gotten to enjoy a vacation before the malfunction on the way home. Gina had thought she would never come to this place, with all the memories and ghosts haunting it, but here she was, waiting for the shuttle to dock and her adventure to begin. She had reached Callista.

As soon as everyone from the shuttle had stowed their belongings into one of the rooms in the only hotel on the planet, a guide led the group of newcomers to the Spectral Fields, since that was what everyone had come to see. He handed everyone a pair of spectral goggles, warning the group not to change the settings yet. Gina slipped hers over her head and instinctively looked at the Fields, as did everyone else. She let out a gasp.

Without the goggles, the Fields was an empty space, with nothing visible to the naked eye except a few occasional flashes of light. In the Spectral Fields, temperatures millions of time higher than humans could tolerate flared against freezing gusts, and sometimes the patterns of temperatures were visible to the naked eye in sparks and explosions. No one knew what the atmosphere was made of in the Field, or how the temperatures were maintained. No one was even sure how it had been found, since the true beauty of the field could only truly be seen through heat-sensitive spectral goggles she was now wearing. And with the goggles, the Fields had come alive.

Where nothing had stood before, now tall grass and human-sized rabbits frolicked and tumbled around. The guide explained that these goggle settings were nearly always a pleasant view of the Fields, but warned that once they started changing the settings they might come across violent and disturbing images.

Gina lifted the goggles, unable to believe her eyes. Without the goggles, the field was empty. She lowered them again and the grass and rabbits were back. Incredible. She would have quite a lot to add to her travel article and mentally she began writing. She wouldn't allow herself to wonder what her parents must have thought about the Fields, whether they had been delighted and satisfied by their choice of vacation.

Gina shook her head and scolded herself. She needed to focus. She was here for work, not sentimentality. The guide hooked them up to a complex system of ropes above their heads, explaining that it was easy to get caught up in the images and lose all sense of reality, so the ropes prevented people from running into each other or, worse, jumping into the Fields. It also prevented them from interrupting the thousands of artists who made their living out on the viewing platform. The tourist ropes were carefully placed so that they could see each artist's work, but not get close enough to interfere. Once they were hooked up, the guide asked them to change the settings.

She reached up to the two knobs on her goggles, one on each side. Changing the settings meant that different temperatures would correlate to different colors in the settings and she expected to see the field and the rabbits again, just in a different hue. Instead, the entire image blurred for a moment before clearing into a familiar scene. It was her parent's house, and to her shock, her mother and father were there, sitting at the kitchen table. They were talking but stopped as the image cleared and the goggle settings finalized. Both of them turned to look at Gina with puzzled expressions on their faces, almost as if they could see her.

Her heart skipped a beat. Her mother was in a pale blue sweater and jeans, and her father was still dressed from a long day at work in a casual suit with his shirt unbuttoned a little at the neck. It looked like he had just come home. She had seen this scene so many times, but had never expected to see it again after the shuttle malfunction took them both away.

Her mother opened her mouth and seemed to say something, but there was no sound in this vision. The two of them stood and left the room, leaving Gina staring at her childhood kitchen in shock. The look in her parents' faces wouldn't leave her. They had seen her, she was sure of it.

She realized with a start that about a week before they left for Callista, they had called her to make sure everything was all right. They had seen a vision of her death and her mother had been so upset she couldn't sleep or eat until they talked to her and knew she was safe. Gina had laughed it off, but what if they had seen her here in the Field? What if the Spectral Field somehow let her shift through time and really be in their kitchen?

She took her goggles off, unable to look at her parents' kitchen anymore. The guide was talking to some of the other newcomers. She asked if it was okay to wander, and he gave her permission. She felt a sense of cold determination fill her. If she had seen her parents once, perhaps she could see them again. After all, the possibilities of the Field were endless. Every different position, every different setting resulted in dramatically different images. She just needed to find a place where she could see them, and the best way she could think of was to wander around and look at the artists' easels until she found an image that looked familiar.

Gina pushed her goggles above her forehead and began to walk, limited by the rope but still able to see the easels of the artists nearby. She was stunned at the variety, and at the different interpretations of artists standing right next to each other. A simple change of the settings, and what was an ocean panorama for one became a scene of mutilation for another. Not a single one bore any resemblance to another, yet they all painted the same scene.

As she walked by the different artists, she pulled her goggles down and tried to find the image they were painting. Often it was easy; they were using the standard setting. But some of them must have been using custom settings because she couldn't see what they were clearly seeing and painting. Just by identifying different temperatures as different colors in the visible light spectrum, the artists could all look at the emptiness and see a world visible only to them.

It was a wonderful feeling, she thought as she roamed and compared the easels to her own vision with the goggles. True power. The smallest touch on the gears, and the entire world shifted into a new order. Creation itself was suspended and rearranged, and the possibilities were endless. The artists could pin the chaos down into a single interpretation, static for the moment and united by the common element driving the artists' vision. Gina preferred her own visions. Not because the shapes or colors were completely different than her vision, although they often were, but because limiting the potential of the Field into a single image seemed counter to the very nature of the Field. A single interpretation didn't matter. The infinite possibilities were what made the Field unique. She was already planning how to phrase this in the travel article. It would be hard, but she could manage it.

One of the artists hunched over an easel was dipping his brush in violent orange, yet the color looked tame against the backdrop of his other strokes. A sense of deadly force emanated from the dire grays and blacks mushrooming from the center of the painting, and Gina could almost make out faint human forms in the smoky paint before the orange slashed and divided them into parts, or perhaps smaller human figures. The pattern seemed endless and the artist's brow was heavy above his goggles as he stared out at the field, then lowered his brush again.

She shuddered. It seemed too much like her parents' death. She didn't look through her goggles for that image, and moved on quickly. Once she was a safe distance away, she noticed an unusual painting and pulled her rope closer so she could study it. Most of the paintings were landscapes, or if they had people in them, the people were viewed from a distance. This one, however, focused on two figures and it stood out among the other paintings. She stayed there for a long time, enjoying the image of a large figure cradling a small, the pinks and blues of comfort and safety and love radiating out.

The soothing colors softened the artist's rendering of a mother and child in a single moment of love, despite the viewer's knowledge that the embrace would have to end eventually. The gentle smile on the larger figure's face seemed aware of this inevitability and Gina marveled at how random jets of hot and cold air could create such detailed human faces and figures.

The guide had explained that the brain was designed to make sense out of chaos and find patterns in nothingness. No matter what it looked like, there were no real figures in the field, he assured them. If they had any doubts, all they had to do was lift the goggles. Apparently, before the rope system was set up, they had experienced problems with people jumping off the platform in an attempt to touch or rescue nonexistent people in the field.

She still had seen nothing of her parents and instead of focusing on the art, she decided to try the goggles again. She slipped the goggles down again and saw the mother and child clearly, but the faces were different than the artist had painted. She gasped as she recognized her mother's features, and her own childish face looking out.

But it was only a moment in time and the scene did not move; her mother didn't look up at the adult Gina, her eyes were fixed on the child in her arms with the same knowing smile that the artist had perfectly captured. Gina fumbled with the settings. This had to work. She had to see her parents, to warn them, find them, see them again. She lowered the right setting and raised the left setting.

The world whirred as the settings changed, and then she was surrounded by turquoise. There were no figures in the image, just turquoise. Then the image seemed to zoom out and she saw her parents strapping themselves into a shuttle. Gina's stomach froze. She knew what was going to happen, but perhaps she could reach them. She waved her arms in the air and her mother frowned and grabbed her father's shirt, pointing at Gina.

"Get off the shuttle," Gina screamed. "You're going to die!"

Her father's brow furrowed and his mouth opened and shut, but she couldn't hear him. They wouldn't be able to hear her, either, she realized. She was just a vision to them; she wasn't there in the flesh even though it felt like it. Her father said something else and a man in a uniform appeared. Her father pointed to her and the man in the uniform paled. The man went to the release door and attempted to open it, but it was jammed. He turned back to her parents with a look of horror on his face and said something she couldn't hear. They unbuckled themselves quickly and her father and the man slammed their bodies against the jammed door.

Gina held her breath. She had read the report. A failed release door had prevented the passengers from leaving, and then a faulty engine had caused the fire that killed them. She couldn't bear to watch but she couldn't look away. She had assumed, and the report had said, that her parents died instantly, but this was not instant. Her parents had known what would happen to them. Her eyes welled with tears but she was barely aware of them. She tried to reach out to her mother, who was wringing her hands with a look of terror Gina had never seen before. But her mother wasn't looking at her anymore; she was looking at the door and her husband.

After several more attempts, the man and her father gave up. Her father turned to her mother and embraced her. Tears ran down both of their cheeks as they kissed. Then a streak of orange appeared and began blossoming into reds and whites before her eyes. The blaze overtook the small chamber in less than a second; her parents' embrace the last thing she saw before everything became fire. A scream filled her ears until strange hands removed the goggles and she realized she had been making the noise. An artist stood with his goggles lifted, her goggles in one hand and a paintbrush dipped in orange in the other. She stared at his painting and recognized it as the scene she had just escaped.

"You see it too?" the artist murmured. His voice was hoarse, and deathly silent after her shriek. "You see, we are all heading that way. It will happen. It has happened. Warn, I must warn. The death, it will happen."

Gina collapsed to her knees and the rope holding her went taut. She had seen her parents' death. The artist continued mumbling as he pressed her goggles into her hands and returned to his painting. She stared at the painting, unable to take her eyes away from the sight of the fire and two blackened figures embracing at the center of the destruction. She was vaguely aware of the guide asking if she was okay. She shoved the goggles into his hands, removed the rope from her waist, and got up, nearly sprinting in her attempt to get off the observation platform and away from the Fields.

Did everyone have visions like hers? Did everyone see lost loved ones, or was it because her parents had died on Callista and some memory of them remained? She had to be the only person to see the images, though, because she couldn't imagine anyone seeing what she had and staying.

Gina tossed the few things she had unpacked back into her bag and dragged it to the port. Images of her parents' death filled her mind but there was only one way off the planet and she was desperate to escape the Fields. She would have to risk a shuttle flight. It would be expensive to leave before her scheduled time and she suspected her news agency wouldn't cover it, because she knew that she would never be able to write about the Fields. She would go down in history as yet one more writer unable to do a travel piece about Callista. Maybe in time, she thought, when the memories had faded. But not now, with the agony of her parents' death so fresh in her mind.

The soonest shuttle was just about to leave and they delayed the takeoff for her because she had a press pass. No one seemed surprised that she was leaving so soon, and she noticed three others who had been on her flight to the planet just that morning. Apparently some people couldn't tolerate the images. And some people grew addicted to them, she thought, remembering the thousands of artists painting the Fields. She shut her eyes and tried to quell the terror she felt at being on a shuttle after just experiencing one explode. When she opened her eyes, she gasped. Her mother and father were standing in front of her.

She looked to both sides but no one else seemed to see them. Gina raised her hands to her face to make sure she hadn't left the goggles on, but her face was clear. Her parents said something but she couldn't hear. Her mother placed her hand over her heart and smiled warmly at her, and her father nodded in the awkward way he did when he told her he loved her. There was no fear or panic in either of them. She studied her father's lips as he said something, and she gasped when she recognized it.

"Come back soon," he said.

Her heart leapt. Were they really here, on Callista? Were their ghosts kept alive in the Spectral Fields, or was this just a delusion?

Gina's face softened into a smile. Her parents were neither in pain nor frightened, and she was reassured to see them so calm after witnessing their death in the fire. She placed her hand on her heart and extended it to them, knowing they would be unable to hear any words of love that she uttered. For a moment she considered staying on Callista to find them again, but she knew it was best if she left. She didn't want to become like the artists, trapped by the images of the Field for the rest of her life. She had a life to live, and now that she had seen her parents happy, she could go back to that life. It was what they would want.

Gina knew her dreams would still be filled with nightmares of her parents' death, but now she had the courage to keep going. Her parents vanished from the shuttle and she relaxed. They were happy and healthy on Callista, and she could visit them whenever she wanted. In time, she knew the pain of their deaths would fade from her memory and only the happy memories would remain. And there were plenty, including this farewell. She looked around to see if any of the other passengers were seeing loved ones, but everyone else had pained expressions and looked like they just wanted to get away. The same way she had looked only moments before. Silently she thanked Callista for allowing her to see her parents one last time, and she vowed to return and see them again as her father had requested.

The shuttle rumbled and took off without any problems, and soon she was headed home. She didn't know what the future held, but she felt comforted that her parents, at least, could be properly laid to rest in her mind and she could move on to that future instead of living in the past.

DESTINY: DNA MESSAGE

He left it in skin cells on subways and rails. In handshakes and kisses and film theater cushions. He left it unknowing, a blind courier; his message went far, round the globe, many said. But only one touch on one glass left its mark, and only one woman could read through the trash. She stared at the message through eons of space, rewriting foundations of humanity's race.

strip junk DNA
down to component atoms
engineer secrets

EARTH: THE WEIGHT OF GOLD

Ambassador Sephir to Galactic Council RE: Earth. 6821 GE
Earth's government remains firm in their decision: they will not accept
our gold offering if they have to give up nuclear weapons. We retrieved
the gold offering and discovered that one or more individuals
unaffiliated with the government had replaced the gold with a variety of
objects. We are unsure how to treat this turn of affairs and have
forwarded you a list of the objects for cultural analysis.

--Report for Cultural Analysis--

Item 1: Two shoes, each three inches long. Believed to be human baby
shoes. Made of animal hide, unsuitable for walking.

Item 2: One plastic necklace with heart-shaped locket. Two photos inside
show male and female human faces.

Item 3: One apparent gold ring with single large diamond. Closer
inspection proved the metal and jewel to be steel and glass.

Item 4: One string of black beads, partially crushed. Possibly a necklace.

Items 5-29: Twenty-four round stones engraved with possible human
writing (language unknown) or human art (style unknown).

Items 30-48: Eighteen bars iron. Impure.

--End Report--

*Item 1: Two shoes, each three inches long. Believed to be human baby shoes. Made of
animal hide, unsuitable for walking.*

The baby's name was Nadir Madari, and he died eleven years before his
shoes were placed in the alien case. He was the first to die from the
Phantom Plague that broke out in cities across the world, killing infants
with bleeding rashes that looked like pinwheels of death on their innocent

skin. It was a new disease and there was no cure. There was no gold to find the cure because the planet was overpopulated; most people viewed the plague as a necessary evil and washed their hands of it.

Those people didn't have to care for the babies the way Khaleel Madari did. He had held his beloved and only son Nadir and watched in horror as the strange rash began and the life bled from his son's body while the child could do nothing but pump his fists in futile rage and scream in terror. Soon, even that was too much and he lay limply, with only occasional wails letting his father know that the baby was still alive. Still suffering.

It was almost a blessing when his son's spirit passed beyond. The feeling of relief upon seeing the relaxation of death on his son's face would haunt Khaleel for the rest of his life. It was a burden no human should carry; relief that one's child has escaped agony through death. He cursed himself every morning and replayed the scene in his mind every night to remind himself of his sin. He had endured the illness, telling himself that Allah punished those He loved best and Allah was testing him to purify his soul of sin. But he had failed in the end. His only son died and he felt relief.

He had left his wife's family, unable to look at her sister's children and unable to see his wife's face and remember the relief in both their hearts as their son's agony ceased. He planned to fade away, vanishing into the underbelly of the city to die childless and alone, without the comfort of family to ease him through the pain. But a dear friend had stopped him and taken him to a community health house where his medical skills and experience were put to use helping other parents cope with the plague.

There was still no cure. The most anyone could hope for was a quick death, and no parent could want a quick death for his or her child and remain sane. He held the children and watched the pinwheels spiral outward on their flesh, and he held the parents and assured them they weren't monsters. The Phantom Plague tore apart the fabric of society and made families frightened and distant, never knowing when someone would have to make that inconceivable choice to let a living, breathing, loving child go. The believers bore the pain and opened their wounded hearts to Allah, but it seemed Allah had turned His back on the world.

The plague struck children at four months of age, after they were old enough to have formed strong bonds with parents, perhaps even old enough to speak the 'mama' and 'papa' that reflected their love. The risk diminished once they learned to walk. No one understood it, and no one tried. Parents started abandoning infants who developed even the slightest rash or fever, convinced it was the plague. Hospitals stopped delivering babies and denied medical care until a child reached its first birthday because the plague was so common inside the city. It was a cruel plague, yet no one looked for a cure. Science, like Allah, shook its head sadly and turned its attention to adults, to the living. To the wealthy.

Khaleel knew there was a cure, if someone were willing to pay. He just needed gold. No families living outside the cities suffered from the plague, for reasons no one understood. Perhaps the diet was better, since he heard they ate cooked food and not ration bars. Perhaps it was access to open air untouched by smog and acid rain. Perhaps it was because they could afford sleeping rooms with less than ten people crowded together, infants crammed between parents' bodies but still in danger of being crushed in the sheer volume of human flesh. Khaleel didn't know, but the plague only hit in the depths of the overflowing cities.

The aliens had given them gold to develop their planet and even if the leaders of the government were too arrogant to accept alien help, he wasn't. He would take their gold and fund research to stop children like Nadir from dying, and perhaps when the aliens returned they would help the humans control their population in ways that didn't involve death. Perhaps they would help humanity finally leave Earth and spread out comfortably. Perhaps, he thought with the last shreds of his devout hope, perhaps they were angels come to bring word of Allah's love at last.

His friend Dolma knew how to access the case with the gold, but she warned that the weight had to be replaced exactly or the government would know it had been taken. Khaleel opened a drawer in his son's old room, now a shrine to the victims of the plague. He removed his son's small shoes and weighed them in his hand.

Nadir had been too young to walk, of course, but Selina – another name too painful to mention – had wanted a picture of them together and bought shoes for her child. He still had the picture of the three of them, smiling happily together, a family. There were no families after the plague. The tiny shoes were so precious to him, but the cure they could buy might save millions. Perhaps that was Allah's plan. Allah was wise and all knowing, and Khaleel was weak to doubt. He kissed his son's shoes and began walking to Dolma's house to arrange the exchange, feeling hope for the first time in a decade.

Item 2: One plastic necklace with heart-shaped locket. Two photos inside show male and female human faces.

The locket was wrapped inside a fancy box with shiny blue edges and a fashionably large bow, and Amali let out a sigh of pleasure as she lifted the adorable necklace high.

"Oh, thank you mommy!"

"Look inside," her mom's static-filled voice said.

Amali was careful to keep her face in the camera range as she slipped her fingernail between the halves of the locket and pushed it open. Two faces smiled at her, one a familiar face, the face looking at her from across the ocean on the monitor right now. The other was foreign but she knew it instantly.

"Is that- dad?"

"Took forever to find. Records aren't what they used to be. But that's him. Jose Guerra."

"Tell me the story again, mommy, tell me the story."

But her mother wasn't able to tell the story of how she met Amali's father that day. Thousands of miles from where Amali sat looking at her father for the first time, an improvised explosive device landed a dozen feet from her mother. The chaos of the explosion and the gruesome results had been displayed for Amali's ten-year-old eyes in crystal clarity.

Fifteen years later and she still remembered the day vividly. She went to counseling and took medicine, as much as her mother's veteran benefits allowed, but it only helped a little. She had no other income and after the doctor's words this morning, she was going to have to find some. But she couldn't use computer monitors. They sent her into a huddled mass of fear. She couldn't see a computer and *not* see her mother's body flung across the room in pieces. And not being able to use a computer was like not having a brain: she couldn't get hired. How could she possibly earn gold?

She ran a finger over the locket and opened it again to look at the warm faces, so young and free. She knew their story intimately, even though she would never hear her mother's velvet voice recite it again. They met in the war, as many couples did. It was the only escape from the cities for most; a welcome opportunity to breathe free air and walk without tripping over living and dead bodies of neighbors.

Because her parents were in the military, Amali had grown up in a boarding house with only eighty other children, and she knew that such privacy was a luxury. She sometimes saw the masses at the camp gates; men and women and children begging to be let in, eyes and cheekbones predatory with hunger, rags barely covering their privates. They weren't healthy enough to join the military, the adults at the base said, so they and their children couldn't enter.

Occasionally Amali would take food to unguarded spots along the perimeter and slip it to the starving kids outside. The outside children, her twins in every way except their parents' choices, would stare at her darkly, hungry for food and opportunity. But there was nothing else she could do.

When Jose and Lisha met, the times were not so dire. The population had not reached its third explosion and war was still something to be avoided rather than an easy way to get rid of excess population. The Phantom Plague was unknown and diseases still had cures.

A lot can change in twenty-six years, Amali thought sadly.

Lisha was stationed in the eastern region of the American Desert in central Texas. The military base was outside one of the few cities still thriving in the desert, several miles from the concrete and asphalt monstrosity that broiled in the heat and looked like a hideous mirage of despair to anyone drawing near.

Once it had been a pleasant city, Lisha said. Her parents – Amali's grandparents – spoke of living there and boating in the lake, and visiting the capital building. But the second population explosion and the encroaching desert forced residents inward and upward like a swarm of ants trapped in a jar with a magnifying glass pointed at the bottom.

The residential towers were built, commerce desperately followed into the depths of downtown, and industry was forced to tail behind after the last oil reserves dried up. The city, and all cities, symbolized what humanity had become: terrified, trapped creatures locked in cages of their own design, unable to leave because the world they destroyed had finally turned against them.

Lisha was an ecological activist, Amali knew. She had only been to a few cities, and not the pretty ones. Her stories were always tainted with bitterness, even her romances.

One night Lisha went to the city on leave, hoping to find someplace in the gray mirage that wouldn't depress her. She wore civilian clothes. A cherry red tank top and high-cropped jean shorts with white sandals, because Amali always asked. The full damage to the atmosphere wasn't known yet, and people didn't cover up properly. Her hair was long then, and curly black.

She went to a bar on 6th Street that didn't look too flashy and had only a few neon signs proclaiming it "The Thirsty Armadillo." She ordered a drink (Amali hadn't been old enough to ask what drink, and the missing detail was a scar in the story) and sat down in one of the booths next to several girls. They were less likely to hit on her, Lisha said with a smile. There were televisions everywhere and on one screen there was a news report.

The extinct species list had been updated to include both remaining species of shark, despite the best efforts of environmentalists. Lisha felt as though her heart had been ripped out. The news wasn't surprising, since most people suspected the animals went extinct years ago, but the confirmation was a knell of doom that she felt deep in her soul.

It was then that she saw a man looking at the same screen with the same expression. He was slightly taller than her, with thick black hair and a smooth face, in a gray short-sleeved shirt with long black jeans. His eyebrows were thick and his eyes were kind and green, like Amali's. His eyes met hers and they fell in love.

"I can't explain it, Amali," her mother always said. "We knew we were soul mates. I stared into his eyes and I knew he was thinking the same as me and I knew he understood me like no one else ever could."

They went on three glorious dates before getting engaged, and she spoke softly about the glow in Jose's eyes when she told him she was pregnant.

"It was hope, Amali. Hope for our planet. Hope that someday things would change and we would find an answer. We have to stop before we destroy ourselves, and you are our answer. We had both lived without hope for so long, but you gave it to us."

Before they could be married, Jose was killed in combat in a war that seemed as unreal as the deaths of the sharks and the mirage city with its millions of people crammed within shrinking walls. Lisha never loved again.

Amali held her locket tightly as she remembered the story, and her mother's face as she told it. Hope. There was no hope anymore. There were only flashbacks and nightmares and her doctor's voice that morning giving her the fatal news.

"You have cancer, Amali. It might be treatable, but the therapy isn't covered by your benefits. Do you have someone who could help you with gold? A friend? A savings account?"

No no no.

"If this isn't treated immediately, your prognosis doesn't look good. One year, maybe two."

The doctor was already dismissing her, already mentally moving on to a patient who had gold to survive. And with so many people in the world, what right did she have to survive? Why Amali and not someone else? Or a dozen someone elses? Because I'm hope, she wanted to say. I'm my parents' hope and if I die, they'll be truly dead and I'll fail them. There had to be an option. There had to be some way to find the gold to survive, no matter what she had to give up.

She had a friend named Dolma who, despite having little gold herself, had spoken about being able to access the gold that everyone knew the aliens had brought to attempt to persuade the governments to give up their nuclear weapons. Dolma would insist on a price, Amali knew, but whatever that price was, she was willing to pay it to keep her parents' hope alive.

Item 3: One apparent gold ring with single large diamond. Closer inspection proved the metal and jewel to be steel and glass.

"What do you mean it's fake?"

Rachel couldn't believe her ears. After everything else that son of a bitch had done, this was the last straw. This ring was the only thing that kept her going, her one hope of escaping the nightmare that was her life. He couldn't take this away, too.

"I mean, it's not gold, and the jewel isn't a diamond. I can't turn it into gold credits for you. It's very well done, though," the jeweler said, turning the ring under his lens. "Even a careful observer wouldn't be able to tell without aid."

"My husband gave this to me at our wedding! It's a family heirloom," she insisted as fear began to clamp down on her vocal cords. "It's the only thing I have left."

The jeweler said nothing but his hazel eyes spoke volumes. Perhaps you should have found a better husband, he seemed to say. She bristled at the silent reproach even while her heart attacked her for the same flaw.

"I have to sell this," she repeated. "My husband left me. I don't have a job. But I'm smart; I went to college. If I can just get a second chance-"

"Everyone needs second chances, lady," he said, but not unkindly. "Look, you seem like you come from wealth. Why don't you go back to your family and ask for help?"

Her lip quivered.

"They kicked me out, not that it's your business. My husband was the wrong religion. Wrong everything," she added under her breath. "I have to sell this. What can you give me for it?"

"Odd to think that religion matters that much to some people. The rest of us are just trying to survive."

She shut her eyes and gripped the counter tightly. Then, with a sigh she was beginning to realize would symbolize her life, she mentally clobbered the nameless terror in her heart and held her hand out for the ring. The jeweler paused, fingering the ring while his other hand moved beneath the counter.

"Did you kill him?" he asked.

She stared at the portly jeweler, whose hand was still under the counter as though poised to summon the police – or as though he were holding a gun.

"Kill who?"

"Your husband. There's a notice linked to the ring. You're wanted by the police."

"He's dead?"

She tried to sound surprised but it was hard. She *was* surprised, though. She hadn't expected anyone to find the body for another day. No one was supposed to visit the house until tomorrow – unless he had arranged a meeting with his mistress. Of course. Of course that bitch would ruin her escape just as she had ruined her marriage. The jeweler was staring at her and she tried to imagine what a guilty person would do. A guilty person would deny it, obviously. She had to do the opposite.

"Good," she muttered. "Giving me a fake ring, abandoning me like this."

The jeweler's hand returned to the top of the counter. "Not bad for a rich kid. I can work with that. What'd he do? Cheat on you?"

"Yes," she cried, slamming her fist on the counter. His hand lowered again but his face was impassive. "He cheated on me, then got my boss to fire me and my friends to abandon me, and he divorced me for that bitch, and-"

Her voice cracked and she began to cry as she reached the unforgivable crime, the act that had pushed her into violence.

"He killed my dog. Hit her while we were walking and then drove away. The cops didn't believe me; he paid them off."

A tissue box appeared from somewhere and she took one gratefully. Another customer entered the store, took one look at her, and backed out. She tried to control her sobs but memories of that dreadful accident flashed through her mind with vicious accuracy. The blood. The exposed bone. And *his* smirk as he drove off. Dogs were endangered but he hadn't even gotten a citation. Gold could do everything; he had it all and she had none.

"Vindictive bastard," the jeweler said in a musing voice. "Well, as long as you have this ring, the cops are going to track you."

She wanted to ask why but she didn't. She knew. Her husband had gold. If he had been a city dweller like the jeweler, the police would shrug and say, "Another rat off the streets." She had heard them say it before when her husband went out drinking with them, eager to go driving through the darkest streets to find a victim so they could feel powerful again. She pretended not to know what they were doing but she knew, and she cringed that she hadn't seen it as a warning sign. Of course he would cheat on her; he was beating and murdering hookers every weekend without apology. But he never loved them, as he claimed to love his mistress. And he had never raised a hand against anyone she cared about.

"If you want to help, then buy the ring," she said, taking a risk that the look in the jeweller's eyes was sympathy.

"The amount I'd give for it would barely cover a night in a ten-room, and even that might be too crowded for a rich kid like you. But it's a heavy ring," he said, hefting it in his hand. "I have a friend, Dolma, who would pay a lot just for the weight. She's putting together some new families, I can see about getting you into one. You have to understand, though, that your current life would be over. You'd have to give everything up, become a new person."

She stared at him, unsure how to react. Ever since her husband had told her about his cheating, confessed as though expecting her to be pleased by his honesty, her life had been sinking further and further into the gutter of the stories she read about in magazines and always felt proud she had managed to avoid. An affair. Divorce. Murder. And now what?

She knew what happened to women who got lost in society's cracks. She knew about the dangers of living in the cities, never breathing fresh air, always packed close with others in a claustrophobic nightmare. A city family: not the loving network she grew up with but a crowded mass of people pooling resources to scrape together enough gold to survive another day. She wouldn't let herself become a victim like millions of other women. But if the police were after her, she needed help. And the jeweler seemed honest enough.

She thought of her current life, her friends who were really *his* friends, her dreams that were really *his* dreams. She thought of her best friend dying in the street as *he* drove away. It wasn't much of a sacrifice.

"What do I do?"

Item 4: One string of black beads, partially crushed. Possibly a necklace.
Items 5-29: Twenty-four round stones engraved with possible human writing (language unknown) or human art (style unknown).

The black beads shifted under Eva's fingers as she whispered prayers and felt her way along the rosary. Dolma knelt beside her, arm around her waist and head bent respectfully. Dolma was an atheist, but a true believer in the sanctity of humanity and she always knelt with Eva for her prayers. Grunts and groans of lovemaking from one of the other couples in the room were ignored with a lifetime of practice. She and Dolma were lucky; they shared an apartment with seven other couples and only four couples slept in each bedroom. Dolma had even managed to claim a corner so they could face the walls and pretend the others didn't exist.

"I'm adding mani stones," Dolma said softly. Eva didn't mind that she spoke; she needed company in the loneliness of her prayers. "From my ancestors. They're heavy, so I'll be able to take a lot of gold from the alien case, and they have prayers from centuries of worshippers in them."

"You're not Buddhist," Eva said between her Hail Mary's.

"I know. But my father wanted me to use them to lead people to enlightenment, and I can't think of a better way. I may not believe but I respect."

Eva gazed at her wife in adoration until the couple writhing on the floor next to them started whispering naughty teases to each other in husky, breathless voices. Aside from the couple entering the throes of passion, another woman slept while her wife completed her nightly self-exam for cancer. The last couple watched television in the common room. Even without staring at the wall, Eva felt alone in the unexpected privacy of the moment.

Their group could afford the luxury space because the location was terrible: one of the lowest floors of a residential tower dead in the city center. They had to constantly reinforce the windows against smog and even with their precautions, they frequently wore masks around the apartment to stave off lung cancer.

Eva and Dolma ignored their group as much as possible, but depended on them too. They were a family. People didn't survive as individuals in the city. None of them were related, which was unusual. Normally blood relatives stayed together, brothers and sisters bringing in spouses and becoming aunts and uncles to hordes of children who soon began producing yet another generation. Families often slept in piles, not having the space to stretch out individually. The piles would thicken until tempers flared too high and quarrelling factions spat out a branch of the family like a child spits out chunks of plastic from the ration bars.

But the eight couples in Eva's apartment had only known each other vaguely before moving in together. They were all female, in the hope that no one would start producing children and send them into poverty. Rape happened, though, and they had already welcomed one daughter only to lose her to the plague. The same woman was pregnant again, raped by her boss again, but Eva ignored it. The only birth control allowed in the cities was death, even though she could remember when all women had the right to control their bodies. Now only the wealthy could afford it. The baby was doomed to be born, and Eva wouldn't let herself become attached until it could walk and the plague couldn't rip it away.

The rosary beads clicked together in her hands as she prayed for a cure to be found, for the mani stones and other offerings to the aliens to accomplish the impossible and save humanity. She prayed every night but deep in her heart she feared her prayers went unheard.

Her grandmother once spoke of a war many generations back, a great war that people had thought was the end of the world. But people survived. In her grandmother's lifetime, people thought things couldn't get any worse and Jesus would return soon. Eva's parents believed the same thing; had prayed that Jesus would come and save them. Her grandmother had spoken of this and looked around at Eva's childhood home: the few inches of space they had to themselves, the orange smoky air outside, the undrinkable gray water in the sink.

"You, Eva," she would sigh. "You are the last. This is beyond humanity's worst nightmare."

Her grandmother firmly believed that God was watching and would save the true believers before the end, but Eva was starting to doubt. When the baby caught the plague, she was reminded of Christ, the innocent lamb sent to the slaughter to atone for the sins of humanity. As she watched the bloody spirals burst open on the child's flesh, though, she realized the comparison was false.

Jesus had been beaten, scourged, and crucified – a horrible, excruciating death. But it was quick. From the time of His arrest to His death on the cross, not even a full day passed. He was tortured, humiliated, placed upon the cross for six hours – and then it ended and He returned to the Heavenly Father's embrace. The child went through the same agony for weeks and when death came, there was no guarantee of grace. She was just another dead baby, not even listed because no one bothered counting children until they reached their first birthday anymore. Why? She had committed no sin. Why had God chosen to torture her? Why did God torture them all?

Dolma's arms circled her and she realized she was crying. It was too much to bear sometimes. Often she held Dolma this same way as the hopelessness of life overwhelmed them. Dolma was strong today, though. She had been strong since the aliens first arrived. The couple nearest them moaned in pleasure as Eva stroked her rosary and held her beloved wife.

"Why are you doing this, Dolma? Taking the gold?"

Eva had her suspicions. Dolma was out of work again after she found out that her latest job disarming nuclear weapons was actually part of a larger plan to learn how to build more efficient ones. She was outspoken in her hatred of the world-destroying weapons but her hatred had also led her to become an expert, so various groups and governments were always manipulating her.

They ignored Dolma's warnings of what a single nuclear attack could do to the planet, to a city with its millions of inhabitants packed tight like a target just waiting to explode. The retaliation would be brutal. Humanity might go extinct. The planet would survive, but it wouldn't be Earth anymore. Eva knew Dolma's predictions and understood that it would be the final apocalypse, but there was little they could do except continue to disarm what they could.

But now the aliens had given them hope and Eva saw it in the energy of Dolma's eyes, the luster of her smile. The aliens would only accept Earth if Earth gave up nuclear weapons. Such a simple request, yet the government refused. So Dolma was accepting the offer of gold on the government's behalf, in her own way, of course.

"The aliens are here to help," Dolma answered. "They gave us the gold to help people. But giving it to the government? Really? They have enough gold. It's the *people* who need the help. I'm just making sure the people get it."

She touched Eva's shoulder and pointed to a necklace with a locket sitting on a nearby bench. "That'll get enough gold to pay for the owner's cancer treatment. It's just over two ounces, but it'll save her life. We're barely making a dent, Eva. There are ten pounds of gold in there and we're not even taking one. Do you have any idea how much even an ounce of pure gold is worth these days?"

She sat cross-legged on their mat and showed Eva the mani stones and how heavy they were.

"With the amount we're taking," she said, "Our family will be able to move up into a home with air, where we won't have to feel for lumps twice a day because the cancer rates are so high. And we'll still have more than enough to feed thousands of people, and house them, and treat them with basic human dignity."

"But why not take it all and have the government find out? Why are you keeping it a secret like this?"

"We have to show the aliens that we aren't all greedy," she said slowly. "And I don't want the government to know because... because I'm sending a message with my objects. The government would never let me send these things. Look what else I'm sending."

Dolma lifted a pair of baby shoes for Eva to see, and a wedding ring. "When the aliens see personal items like this, they'll understand that the *government* may refuse their offer, but we the people are desperate for their help. They won't refuse such intimate offerings. Surely they can't ignore us when we're giving them our memories and souls. They can't leave us here to die from the government's greed."

Eva stroked the beads around her neck. She had been thinking for days and had finally made a decision. Dolma's mani stones had given her courage.

"Dolma, I want to add something."

"What is it?"

She removed the rosary hesitantly. She had never been without it since her grandmother placed it on her head and whispered a prayer of blessing before gratefully ascending to Heaven. Her grandmother often said the future of humanity rested in the beads of the rosary. Eva knew she didn't mean it literally; she meant the future rested in religion, in Christ's sacrifice, but often Eva liked to believe that she actually held the fate of the world in her loving hands as she recited prayers, imagining each bead a different person in the world that she protected and cared for. Eva clung to the rosary now, terrified to let the beads out of her fingers.

"I want the aliens to know us, as a people. I want them to have this. I don't want the gold. Give the gold to someone who needs it. But please, give them this."

Dolma's eyes filled with tears as she took the rosary reverently. She knew how significant it was, what a sacrifice Eva was making. Dolma had been one of the beads ever since she and Eva fell in love years ago. Dolma wasn't religious, but Eva liked to think that her grandmother would approve of her granddaughter's choice of wife. She liked to think her grandmother would approve of her choice to send the rosary to the stars as well. It was, after all, the only hope of survival humanity had left.

"I will, Eva," Dolma said. "I know they will cherish this as much as you do. Our offerings may be small, but they have a meaning anyone can recognize, alien or human."

Eva felt naked without the rosary as she kissed her love, but she felt safe in the knowledge that the aliens wouldn't be blind to Dolma's message. The aliens seemed to follow Christ's path, after all, in trying to ease the suffering of strangers. God willing they would see beyond the corruption and find the true believers among the humans, and lift them from darkness. The governments might still want their weapons and wars, but the people were weary, and the people of Earth welcomed the aliens and their terms of alliance with open arms.

Items 30-48: Eighteen bars iron. Impure.

What the hell *was* this crap? Where was the gold? Hector shoved a plastic necklace out of the way – plastic, for Christ's sake! – and found the gold in the back of the case. Thank God. It was mostly there, behind a pile of rocks. Rocks! He was careful not to disturb the careful weight balance but he was tempted to rip out all the trash and smash it into a million pieces. Someone had gotten here first. Several someones, from the looks of it.

Hector couldn't believe their arrogance. By all rights the gold was his. Who was to say the aliens hadn't stolen it from his family, after all? It was awfully suspicious. Ten pounds of gold, magically appearing from the sky exactly twenty years after an identical amount had been stolen from his grandfather and sent his family from the height of opulence into the dreaded city; his grandfather's wings melting in the sun of some rival's greed.

The change in fortune had cost his grandfather his life, and his grandmother hers. They didn't even have graves he could visit; they had been collected like goddamn garbage from the ghettos. Their bodies had been tossed in the waste disposal plant with hundreds of other street casualties, incinerated to pump electricity into the city's veins and feed the hungry monstrosity another day. And Hector's parents, though alive, might be better off dead.

They lived in a community health house now and stared at the television blankly with dozens of other mindless drones, unable to process their new environment. Sometimes they recognized him, but mostly they asked in vague terror why so many people surrounded them, and the nurses had to subdue their agoraphobia with drugs. Hector rarely visited anymore.

He stared at the bars of iron he had placed on the ground. He had brought enough to replace all the gold in the container but now he would only be able to use some of them. Glaring at the rubbish in the alien case, he cautiously removed the first gold bar. He waited for a moment, hoping against hope that the gold would replace itself like Fortunatus' purse. The warning light turned yellow at the weight imbalance and Hector added iron bars equaling the same as the gold. The light returned to green as the weight leveled out. As long as the transaction took less than thirty seconds, the alarm would remain silent.

Hector swore under his breath. When he had stumbled upon the idea of replacing the gold with iron, he had felt like Einstein connecting energy and mass in a revolutionary new way. And when he managed to hack the case's controls and persuade it to open, he had assumed it was because he was a brilliant hacker despite his lack of experience. He was good at everything he did; why would hacking be any different? But now he was beginning to think that manipulating the case's controls was easy because someone else had done it first, and perhaps he wasn't as clever as he had thought.

No. That was ridiculous. Of course he was clever. This just meant that someone else in the world was clever, too, and with so many billions of people he shouldn't feel upset. But this was going to be his great accomplishment, the untamed bow that would yield only at his touch and mark him as king, returning him to the seat of power that was his birthright. He hoped to God that whoever had stolen his gold would die a violent, nasty death. He was the only one who deserved this wealth. He had suffered patiently in the service of others, denied the wealth that should have been his, and now it was his turn to claim his reward and carefully sow the seeds of prosperity. The rest of the world could go to hell for all he cared.

He was rich enough now to live in a compound outside the city, but he still shared a cramped six-room with five other men, and frequently their girlfriends as well, even though they had agreed not to bring any additional people into the apartment. Whenever he had a girlfriend, he made sure to spend the nights at her place, unless she lived in the city. If she did, he reluctantly brought her back home, introduced her, and hoped no one would "mistakenly" start making out with her in the middle of the night.

Twice now he had awoken to his girlfriend moaning under his roommate's bulk and both times the bitch appeared genuinely surprised it wasn't him. His roommate wasn't surprised, though, and never tried to fake it. The sneaky bastard planned it all, and snuck quickies with everyone's girlfriends when they weren't watching.

He was sick of it. Sick of waking up hungry for a girl only to find her with someone else, the jealousy burning his chest as they rocked back and forth like a fucking pendulum beside him. Or on the nights he was alone, waking to find everyone else in the room satisfying themselves and mocking his arousal, feeling like the ground was shrinking beneath his feet as one of the women might laugh and ask her boyfriend if Hector could join, just this once, she felt so sorry for the poor kid. People were not meant to live like this. They had become animals.

He wanted his childhood again, when he and his brother had a room to themselves, his two cousins next door, and his parents in yet another room, alone to share their romance and secrets in private. Privacy, the noblest of virtues, which had been stripped away in the blink of an eye when his grandfather's house was invaded by black-clad strangers measuring and moving objects as Hector's parents clung to him and tried to explain that things were changing, they were going to the city now but it was alright, they would be alright, repeating the words in a sickening sing-song designed to persuade themselves more than anyone else.

He remembered his grandfather and grandmother that first night in the city weeping and weeping together while all around them hundreds of other people ate and drank and fucked and shat mere inches from his precious family. Hector had closed his eyes against the pandemonium and he didn't see his grandparents gasp for air, or turn blue. He didn't see the nightly checkers haul their bodies away without a word, ignoring my parents' demand that they be buried, or acknowledged, or... something. Anything. He didn't see, but he heard, and he didn't forget.

He cursed at a rosary that lay coiled in the alien case where gold should have been. How dare some religious zealot play games like this. God had abandoned the world long ago and left them shattered and soulless. Even Satan rejected them, appalled at what humanity had done with its free will. The only thing worth living for was gold, and this time Lady Fortune would give him his due. He dropped a bar of iron on the rosary, deliberately crushing the cross and many of the beads in his anger. The light turned yellow at the sudden weight but returned to green as he removed more gold.

He was furious that people had taken his treasure but tried to console himself with thoughts of what was left. His roommates and coworkers would all wonder at his sudden wealth, of course, at the personal home he would be able to afford – inwardly he gloried at the extravagance of an entire house filled with milk and honey and gold, serving no purpose except to please him – but they would never suspect, because the case would return to the aliens with the same weight inside, seemingly unopened. Only he would know otherwise.

His lips twisted into an ugly scowl. He and a bunch of greedy fools. He replaced a third bar of gold, and a fourth. Those were the only remaining gold bars. The rest was made of smaller pieces and they were no longer neatly arranged. He had counted on being able to take out the pieces and replace them with bars of iron, but it appeared the other idiots who had left their garbage had taken the gold in the chaotic, meandering carelessness of three men in a boat and now there was no clear way to tell the weights of the scattered pieces without removing them. He would have to work quickly and pray for the best.

Hector sweated heavily as he took out gold pieces to match the weight of the iron bar, one eye on the warning signal and one on the scale, and yet somehow a third on the gold because his hands were slick and he was terrified of dropping it and sounding the alarm. The warning signal flashed to yellow many times, but never slipped into red.

He had to leave several pieces of gold regretfully, but he didn't think they were enough to balance out with an iron bar and his heart was pounding too hard to try. Nine pounds of gold would have to be enough. He grinned. That much gold, in such a pure state, would make him one of the wealthiest men in the country. He would buy back his family estate and then some. He had wandered through the woods and stumbled upon Lady Fortune at last.

He carefully packed his treasure into the padded shoulder bag and hefted his pounds of gold. He thought of his parents staring at the television and his grandparents' ashes exhaled into the smog of the city. He couldn't help them, but he could make sure his children never felt the terror and mind-numbing apathy he had endured. There was still hope for them. He would buy a home, and find a wife. They would have a family and live in privacy the way God intended, not like the beasts inhabiting the city in human form. He thought of the rocks the other fools had left and laughed. Let them have their few ounces of gold. He would become king of his private domain, and the world would never touch him again.

Ambassador Sephir to Galactic Council RE: Earth. 6824 GE

Three galactic years have passed since our gold offering. We continue to await the cultural analysis report and we continue to stress the need for immediate results. If even a small portion of the population is willing to accept our terms, we have a galactic duty to protect them. We request that analysis of the case be given the highest priority, as extinction of the species seems imminent.

Ambassador Sephir to Galactic Council RE: Earth. 6826 GE

We regret to inform the Council that a large-scale nuclear war has resulted in mass human, animal, and plant casualties and made living conditions significantly worse for all remaining organisms. Given the continued lack of results from cultural analysis, we consider the matter of Earth closed. We will leave an observation drone and return to incorporated space pending further instructions.

ACRON: APOCALYPSE

smoke fog ash debris
coating ground buildings trees
crowds now silenced, empty beach
countdown ended; time run out
one mustn't say bodies

single searchlight pierces dark
cast upon the snow of ash
forsaken shadows lengthen, leap
tread upon the godless night
one mustn't say chaos

palm trees stark against the night
lifeless malls lie desolate
cracks and bursts explode mid air
ground erupts in dancing fire
one mustn't say despair

a trail of speech pervades the ash
flee the city, track the voice
somewhere is daylight
somewhere is life
one must say hope

TOPSIDAE II: ROADSIDE ETHICS

My first reaction when I saw the baby 'ceratops at the roadside tourist trap was the same as any five-year-old child's and is the reason ecotourism works, but also the reason scum like these men still survive. Topsidae II, in the Creta system, was a miracle of parallel evolution, and the men just outside the city gates had five baby 'ceras, each in a small pot of water barely big enough to hold them. Aside from the creatures' miniature size and the fact that they preferred semi-aquatic living to grasslands roaming, the 'ceras were nearly identical to the triceratops of Old Earth who roamed the imaginations of human children.

I recognized most of the baby 'ceras: the classic three horn, the proud single horn, and two of the common two-horns. The last was a type I had never seen before, sporting an elaborate frill with holes in it, too elaborate to be from an injury. I wondered if it was one of the geneticist's specialty pets that had been abandoned (or stolen) from the ultra-wealthy who wanted a dinosaur of their own.

I didn't want to stop at the roadside exhibit. I try to promote animal rights all the time. I watch eSpecials about how to protect wildlife and stop poaching and smuggling all the time, and I donate to wildlife preservation on my home planet every month. I knew that since the government decided to decrease the level of oxygen in the air to make it less flammable and more tolerable to humans, the 'ceras had been listed as endangered and the price for their horns, organs, and babies had skyrocketed. I knew that these poor babies had probably seen their parents murdered and butchered for body parts by the same men who now put them in pots and earned a living amusing idle tourists too impatient to go into the forest and see a real 'cera. I knew their lives were miserable and tormented, and once the babies stopped making money they would be killed for their own body parts or sold as pets to irresponsible owners who would mistreat and abuse them.

I always thought if I saw something like this I'd call the cops and report it, but here on Topsidae it was well-known that the local police got kick-backs from poachers, so telling them about the illegal operation would be useless. It might even get me arrested and I couldn't get arrested or I'd lose my new job on Topsidae's moon. On the eSpecials I watched, there were always people undercover and the animals often got rescued, and I wished I had a way of contacting those groups and telling them about the babies.

I wondered if I could buy the babies and turn them over to a watchdog group. It would be far outside my price range; would I be compensated? But if I waited to ask about compensation, the babies would be long gone. An impulse buy would convince the men that I wasn't a galactic cop, right? I knew the men needed to be put in jail but I would rather see the babies rehabilitated and returned to the wild while they were young enough to have a chance.

But I couldn't afford to buy even one unless I got some sort of compensation. I'd only gotten out of college the year before and I'd be paying off debts from the institute and travel back and forth to my parents' world for the next decade or so, even though my new job on Topsidae's moon paid better than most of my classmates'. That was, of course, assuming I didn't get married or buy a condo or lightcar. Then I, like most other citizens, would be in debt so long I'd never get out. No, as much as I wanted to buy one or more of these babies and promptly give them to the Cera Sanctuary we were headed to in the afternoon, I could never afford it and I didn't have the time or resources to find out if there was a program to help people in my situation. I was trapped.

I knew that stopping at these roadside amusements promotes inhumane treatment of animals, promotes poaching and enslavement and a whole way of life I find despicable. But I was walking into town with two new friends from work on our first visit to the planet and it was hard to avoid, and besides I felt drawn to the babies despite my inability to buy them or report them or help them in any way. My new friends stared at the babies and I envied their ignorance as the men gave a spiel about how valuable and protected the 'ceras were. The men offered to let us feed the one with holes in her frill – for a fee, of course.

She was very similar to the 'ceras without horns, except for the elaborate pattern of holes. She was the center of everyone's attention, naturally, since she was the most unusual of the unusual animals, and a sign by her pot proclaimed her to be part of a rare and relatively unknown subspecies. That confirmed my suspicion that she was probably designed by a geneticist to have a lattice-like frill, then tossed at the lab or snatched on the way to her new home. It occurred to me, though I didn't dwell on it, that the men might have sawed into her frill when she was an infant and made the design themselves. If they did it early, while the bone was still relatively soft and her skin still growing, it would result in the reasonably smooth and unscarred appearance she now had. I stared at her big black eyes and prayed that some careless rich person had just wanted a specialty dinosaur.

My friends decided that I could feed the dinosaur and despite myself I was grinning foolishly, my hands trembling with excitement. I wanted to blame it on the high oxygen in the atmosphere but knew it was the thought of getting within inches of a real, live 'cera. My friends knew how much I loved dinosaurs; I had spent the entire shuttle from the moon talking about 'ceras and how much I wanted to see one in the wild. They probably didn't even realize the ethical consequences of this roadside atrocity and only thought it would make me happy. And damn it all, I was happy. The oxygen wasn't helping; I felt giddy.

The men gave me chunks of a melon-pineapple fruit shaped like a large kidney bean, one of the few things 'ceras ate. Under their beaks, 'cera's mouths were specifically designed to suck in the yassa fruit whole. Most chewed it, but I knew that these babies, and adults unlucky enough to be caught by slavers, had their teeth removed and sold. They inhaled the fruit and had to let it digest in their bellies whole, causing all sorts of pain and eventually stomach cancer if they lived long enough.

The baby looked at me like a flower out of the pot, staring straight into my eyes as she lowered her jaw into the uniquely bean-shaped opening. Using the provided scoop, I slid one yassa in, trying my best to make the fruit fit the opening. It was harder than I thought and it went in crooked but she didn't mind and slurped it down before opening again. The next one missed her mouth completely, my hands shook so much, and the yassa fell into the water barely visible around her plump torso. The men laughed and told my friends it was much harder than it looked, and as they fished the fruit out I saw feces and what looked like bones from another 'cera underneath the baby's feet. The third fruit went in perfectly and everyone cheered. I tried to remember how often 'ceras ate, because she seemed stuffed after two beans and the men had given me three to feed her, but she was also a baby and presumably needed to grow.

"How often do you feed them?"

"One visitor per group, three pieces," the man said, smiling.

"But how much per day?"

"Oh, they are very healthy, very healthy. See how shiny her eyes are? We give vaccines every month and a pound of food every day."

I doubted any of the babies weighed more than five pounds and I tried to school my expression so my horror didn't show. They were stuffing the babies, probably so they would grow faster, and for the first time I realized that the babies were being kept intentionally immobile because they were likely going to be sold as meat in the city. They were being stuffed and kept from exercise, and in the meantime paraded around as if they were beloved children.

"Why so many vaccines? Is that safe?"

The other men were not smiling as brightly now and I realized I was asking too many questions. They were beginning to think I was a galactic cop, or undercover.

"We have many diseases from tourists. We protect our little 'ceras."

"That's smart," I forced myself to say.

The female 'cera pinned me with velvet black eyes as my friends lavished donations. I pulled out a five-spot. It wasn't so much money that I would look guilty or suspicious, I decided, but enough to reflect the pleasure of seeing real live 'ceras up close. I didn't want them calling the cops on me, because the cops would retrieve my file and circulate my name even if I paid enough to prevent an arrest. And just the hint of criminal activity on Topsidae was grounds for termination at my new job. With a dirty record and no job, I would have no income, little chance of finding a new job within the Creta system, and no money to travel elsewhere. I had no choice but to smile and give the man my money and thank him.

But giving it to the man was a betrayal of everything I stood for and I paused slightly when taking it out of my wallet, wondering if I would have the courage to ask whether the baby was for sale, already knowing she was not, not for me at least, wondering if I could bear to live with myself for supporting these men and leaving this beautiful infant in their hands to be fattened and slaughtered for some bastard's lazy pleasure, already knowing I would bury this memory deeply and never think of it again, knowing that my head would never be held as high and my dreams would never again be free. She would haunt me and I deserved to be haunted. I gave the man my money and left with my friends. I didn't look back. And I didn't cry.

ABOUT THE AUTHOR

Anne Elizabeth Winchell is an author, gamer, artist, and teacher. She grew up in Spokane, Washington and began writing speculative fiction in elementary school. Her passion for science fiction and fantasy led her to Texas State University, where she earned an MFA in Creative Writing and went on to teach creative writing and video game studies. In her spare time, Winchell designs and sells 3D digital models for use in art, film, and video games.